Paint the Wind

Paint the Wind

PAM MUÑOZ RYAN

SCHOLASTIC PRESS NEW YORK

Library of Congress Cataloging-in-Publication Data

Ryan, Pam Muñoz.
Paint the wind / by Pam Muñoz Ryan. — 1st ed. p. cm.
Summary: After her overprotective grandmother has a stroke, Maya, an orphan, leaves her extremely restricted life in California to stay with her mother's family on a remote Wyoming ranch, where she discovers a love of horses and encounters a wild mare that her mother once rode.
ISBN-13: 978-0-439-87362-8   ISBN-10: 0-439-87362-2
[1. Self-actualization (Psychology) — Fiction. 2. Ranch life — Wyoming — Fiction.
3. Family life — Wyoming — Fiction. 4. Horses — Fiction. 5. Wild horses — Fiction.
6. Orphans — Fiction. 7. Wyoming — Fiction.] I. Title.
PZ7.R9553Pai 2007   [Fic] — dc22   2007000854

10 9 8 7 6 5 4 3   08 09 10 11

Printed in the United States of America
First edition, September 2007
The display type was set in PT Vincent Regular.
The text type was set in Perpetua.
Book design by Marijka Kostiw

To my sister,

Sally Gonzales,

for her determination

and courage to

walk, jog, lope, gallop . . .

one step at a time

— P.M.R.

In present-day English grammar, the pronouns *he, she,* and *who* are not commonly used to describe nonhuman beings. I employed them in my story to recognize the animals as integral characters and to honor my own heartfelt sentiments and those of many people for our pets and wild friends.

Thank you

Bobbie and Mike Wade of High Wild & Lonesome wilderness outfitters, for my seven-day ride in southwestern Wyoming. And to my fellow horsewomen: Dawn, Ellen, Ginny, Helen, Kate, and Sally — for their camaraderie.

Dana Rullo at Dana Rullo Stables, Olivenhain, California, my stellar and wise riding instructor and friend. And to Mary Leigh for reviewing the manuscript.

Dave Dohnel at Frontier Pack Train Packing Station, outfitter for my four-day ride in the eastern Sierras. And to Shelley for going with me.

Gilcrease Museum, The Museum of the Americas, Tulsa, Oklahoma.

Ginger Kathrens, author of *Cloud: Wild Stallion of the Rockies* and executive director of the Cloud Foundation.

Hope Ryden, author and photographer of the prestigious works *America's Last Wild Horses* and *Wild Horses I Have Known,* for reviewing the manuscript with consummate attention.

Joyce Herbeck, Ed. D., Montana State University.

Kathy Johnsey and the Pryor Mountain Wild Mustang Center, Lovell, Wyoming.

Neda DeMayo, founder of Return to Freedom, the American Wild Horse Sanctuary, Lompoc, California.

Roland Smith, author, zoologist, friend.

Scott Sutherland, owner of Smokem, Jr. ("Smokey"), my training horse.

Tracy Mack, visionary editor. And Jean Feiwel and Liz Szabla, pathfinders.

When I bestride him, I soar, I am a hawk.

He trots the air. The earth sings when he touches it.

The basest horn of his hoof is more musical than the pipe of

Hermes. . . . He is pure air and fire . . . the prince of palfreys.

His neigh is like the bidding of a monarch, and his countenance

enforces homage.

William Shakespeare, *Henry V*

Dum vivimus vivamus.

Let us live while we live.

Latin Proverb

Walk

1

ARTEMISIA KNEW IT WAS TIME TO DROP THE FOAL.

All afternoon she had felt restless and had paced on the periphery of the band of wild horses. She paused only to graze, but without her usual interest. The sky grew dusky and she stopped chewing altogether, grass still dangling from her muzzle as if she'd forgotten there was food in her mouth. In recent weeks, her udder had swollen but she had grown accustomed to the tight soreness. Now, her nipples waxed with small beads of first-milk.

With the promise of darkness, she wandered from the others, her brown-and-white tobiano markings swaying with the cumbersome passenger inside. Artemisia heard the gentle nickering of the horses she left behind: Mary, her daughter; Georgia, her "sister" mare; Wyeth, Georgia's two-year-old colt; and Sargent, the palomino stallion who had sired the offspring.

Before she disappeared over a sage-covered hill, she glanced back and saw Sargent's protective stare and stance: head raised, ears twisting in her direction, front legs braced, as though he were questioning her exit. He whinnied. She answered with a low guttural nicker. She knew that he could not help her now, nor would he follow her. Artemisia had to face the birth alone, armed only with the instincts of her ancestors.

She lumbered forward with a familiar apprehension. The birth of her first foal had been successful. Mary was a strong and healthy two-year-old. But the memory of last year's foal still burdened Artemisia. The baby had never risen and stayed lifeless on the ground. Artemisia had kept vigil for several days, often touching her muzzle to the small body and hoping for a miraculous change. She had finally returned to the band of horses, alone and despondent, her head dropped low. Would tonight's foal suffer the same fate?

Artemisia found a cluster of high sage and rabbitbrush and lay down within it. Unsatisfied, she soon stood to paw at the ground and walk in a circle. Her flanks perspired. Only after she felt the gush of water and knew the birth was imminent did she stay prone. With each contraction, her huge head and neck arched backward and her long legs stiffened. As she pushed the foal closer to birth, her breathing became deep and heavy. The amniotic sac appeared, and through the taut pearly film, a hoof could be seen, and then another and the promise of the muzzle, as if the foal were poised in a diving position. Artemisia moaned and grunted. The head and shoulders emerged and, as the upper body of the foal delivered, the filmy membrane separated.

Artemisia raised her head, straining to glimpse her newborn.

The foal lay limp, half in and half out of this world, still nothing more than a ghost of a possibility.

2

MAYA'S VIOLET EYES WIDENED, HER VOICE BREATHLESS
with conviction. "The only way to capture a ghost is to
paint the tail of the wind."

With one hand, she picked up the small brown-and-
white plastic horse and moved it in swift arcs over the
chenille bedspread. The June sun eased a notch lower in
the southern California sky and flooded through the
west windows of the two-story house where she lived
with Grandmother. Maya made the figure prance through
the shimmering air and whispered, "I am a mysterious
phantom, belonging to the stars. Who will find me?"

With the other hand, she chose a black stallion and
swept it upward after the ghost horse. She raced the
black horse forward and said, "I am riding the wind,

5

faster than fast. *I* am coming for you." The black horse overtook the ghost. "You're mine forever!" she said, pairing the figures in one hand and sweeping them above her head.

The toy Arabians, Paint horses, Appaloosas, and assorted breeds that spilled from a shoe box had once belonged to her mother. Back then, the colors had been true: sorrel, bay, buckskin, grulla, palomino, and dun. Years of handling with playful caresses had erased their vibrant hues, and now only a memory of paint remained.

Maya was only five when her parents died. Since the accident six years ago, she had lived with her grandmother on her father's side. She didn't remember much about her mother, except for the things Grandmother told her. That her mother was too outspoken for her own good. That she'd never made any effort to blend with refined Pasadena society. And that her place should have been in the home and not traipsing all over kingdom-come on a horse. Maya suspected there were more important things to tell. Beautiful things like the tiny snippets of memory that sometimes flashed in her mind: Mother singing to her at bedtime, her face so close that her long hair tickled Maya's cheeks. Or the one vivid memory Maya cherished: she and her mother, sitting in a tiny windowed alcove in a room with a crooked ceiling, playing with these very figures. Her mother *had* told her about ghost horses and how they lived wild, running free and belonging only to the stars. Hadn't she?

Maya took a photo from the bottom of the shoe box and stared at the glossy image. Her mother sat on a brown-and-white horse, reins in one hand, the other hand waving. And she was laughing, her smile broad and full, her eyes dancing with joy and affection.

The young woman in the photo could have been Maya in a few years. They had the same delicate and lean frame, russet-red hair, and unforgettable purplish eyes. The difference was Maya's skin, a shade darker in tone and suggesting her father's and grandmother's southern European roots.

Maya turned the photo over. Pasted on the back was a tiny section of a page that had been clipped from a book of baby names and their meanings. She reread the entry between May and Maybel.

Maya. A journey about to begin.

She carried the photo of her mother and the brown-and-white horse to the front window of her bedroom.

As usual, she arranged the figure and the picture on the sill so that they faced the street. She stood behind them with her hands clasped, looking out too, as if they were all onlookers at a parade.

From this perch, she had a good vantage of Altadena Lane with its long sidewalks and procession of giant oaks. Manicured yards stretched between wide driveways. Fuchsia bougainvillea burdened most fences. Hydrangea bloomed with lavender flowers the size of dinner plates. But Maya looked beyond it all. She tried to imagine everything that the tiny horse knew about her mother that Maya did not: a life far, far away from Pasadena, filled with stallions and mares, leather reins, boots, saddles, and unrestrained joy. What had made her mother so happy? Maya wondered if her own laugh echoed her mother's. Her face clouded. She'd long forgotten the sound of her mother's laughter and, besides that, she couldn't remember the last time she'd heard her own, either.

With a sudden *cluck*, the bedroom door opened.

Maya whirled around.

The new live-in housekeeper, Morgana, walked into the room. She had been employed for only a week, was conscientious to a fault when it came to pleasing Grandmother and, at least for now, was Grandmother's ardent ally. Even so, Maya knew it was just a matter of time until she joined all the others who had left in a determined huff or sobs of tearful relief. Once, Maya had tried to remember all the housekeepers she had known since she came to live with Grandmother, but she lost count at eighteen.

"Just checking on how your homework is progressing," said Morgana. She was skinnier, older, and nosier than most. Wearing the mandatory black dress and white apron, with her dark hair pulled back into the requisite snood at the nape of her neck, she looked like a wrinkled, malnourished penguin.

Morgana stared at the toy horses on the bed. "Maya, your grandmother was very specific about how your day is to be structured. I escort you to and from school. Afterward, you are to do homework until dinner at six. No playing." She raised her eyebrows.

Maya gave her a sweet smile. "I already finished my homework. And I get straight A's. So you don't actually need to check on me. The other housekeepers didn't. We made an agreement: I come down to dinner on time, and they leave me alone in my room. As long as my grades are absolutely perfect, Grandmother doesn't mind."

Morgana tensed. "I think you'll find I'm not like other housekeepers. I take my job seriously, and since your grandmother pays my wages, which are three times what I'm used to receiving, I'll be considering her wishes, not yours. To be quite honest, it's refreshing to find an employer who shares my vision about how children should be monitored."

Maya sighed. She knew the type. Morgana might last a little longer than most, but not much.

Morgana nodded toward the horses. "I'm quite sure your grandmother would not approve of that kind of idleness."

Maya looked up at her with doe-eyed innocence. "I'm really sorry. I like to play with these once in a while to remember my mother. She gave them to me . . . you know . . . *before*."

Morgana's demeanor softened. "Oh. Yes, your grandmother mentioned that. How did they . . . ?"

Maya's eyes widened. "It was six years ago and awfully tragic. We were on vacation in Costa Rica at a very fancy resort. You see, they took me to someplace exotic every year, just the three of us. Paris, Hawaii, you name it. We went snorkeling in this beautiful crystal-clear lagoon. We were all holding hands and happily swimming and looking at the gorgeous tropical fish and the coral reefs. Then, we began following a giant sea turtle. My mother had always dreamed of swimming with sea turtles. But before we knew it, we were out too far and a motorboat didn't see us in the water." Maya swept her hand through the air. "And it came racing across the lagoon . . . *Swoosh!*"

Morgana put one hand on her chest.

"It was frightening. At the very last second, my father picked me up and tossed me out of the path of the boat and saved my life. But sadly for my parents, the unimaginable happened. . . ."

Morgana moved a hand to her face.

Maya picked up the horse from the windowsill, blinked out a few tears, and sniffled. "The little horses are the only things I have left of my mother, but I keep them hidden from my grandmother, out of politeness. Grandmother has an uncontrollable fear of horses. It's extremely intense and brings back all sorts of ghastly memories from a long time ago when she was thrown from a dangerously wild stallion. She gets awfully angry at anyone who even brings up the subject. You won't mention them, will you?"

Morgana stared at Maya with pursed lips. "Put them away, Maya. And don't be late for dinner."

After Morgana left, Maya scowled at the closed door. The horses and the photo *were* the only things Maya had left of her mother. That part was true. But could Morgana see through the rest of her lies? Would she betray her? Maya scolded herself for making such an egregious error. She should never have taken her toy horses from their hiding place around someone as untested as a new housekeeper.

Maya replaced all the horses and the photo and took the shoe box to the closet. She stuffed it inside a jacket, which had been zipped almost to the top and tied snug at the waist with a drawstring. Then she checked the closet for any signs of disarray. Everything seemed to meet Grandmother's requirements: cotton skirts, prim dresses, and the most recent plaid school uniform all hung equidistant from one another. Every hanger and collar aligned in the same direction. The toes of her shoes pointed forward in regimented formation. Tomorrow's white blouse hung on the back of the door, washed and ironed by Morgana.

Maya glanced into the mirror opposite the bed. She smoothed her hair into slick compliance and tied it in a ponytail. She examined her pleated skirt and crisp blouse for lint and checked her thin white socks to make sure they were folded over exactly two inches. Maya thought them ridiculous and outdated. But what did it matter anyway? So few people saw her. Maya rubbed at a smudge on her left patent-leather shoe until her finger was hot and raw. Grandmother hated smudges.

The clock inched toward six o'clock. Slowly, Maya walked downstairs. On the wall opposite the banister, a dozen photos of her father, each the same size and with identical wood frames, descended in precise increments: first baby pictures, then elementary school, graduations from high school and college, and events where he wore business suits and tuxedos, all with Grandmother on his arm. The last photo had been taken in a studio: Father, Grandmother, and Maya when she was a toddler. Father held her in his lap, and her chubby baby hand reached up and touched his face. Grandmother stood behind him with both hands planted firmly on his shoulders. Maya had long stopped asking about her parents' wedding picture or any photo of her mother. The only evidence that her mother had existed was the snapshot hidden in the shoe box. And the ghostlike suggestions of her presence in photos from which Grandmother had clipped away her image.

In the dining room, Maya tiptoed to her chair at the table, careful not to upset the mahogany sideboard with its display of milk-glass vases. The white damask seat cushions had been covered in clear plastic, as was all of the upholstered furniture in the house. Maya slipped into her chair, smoothed her skirt behind her legs, and sat on it squarely, hoping to avoid the stickiness of plastic on skin.

Morgana entered, positioned herself in front of the kitchen door, and surveyed the table.

Maya's eyes did the same. Everything appeared in order: white linen napkins one inch from the edge and folded with the creases to the left. Water pitcher sitting on a triangular folded tea towel with the handle positioned to the right. Maya couldn't find one viola-tion, not even a wrinkle on the white brocade tablecloth. She breathed a tiny sigh of disappointment. Morgana was good.

The hall clock chimed six.

Maya folded her hands in her lap and waited.

3

ARTEMISIA PAUSED BETWEEN CONTRACTIONS, PANTING
and knowing there would be more. Soon she felt the pressure of
the fierce cramping and bore down until the slippery foal slid
completely into the world.

When Artemisia stood, the umbilical cord broke. She
dropped her head and licked the baby's damp and clotted fur,
her tongue persuading him to breathe. At last, he twitched
and stirred. The small body roused. The foal, who would become
known as Klee, rolled onto his chest, lifted his heavy, wobbly
head, and perked his ears. Minutes later, he stood but braced
his front legs too far apart. He collapsed on the ground, limbs
splayed like bird wings. Artemisia waited until he rose again,
stiff-legged and tottering. She moved closer, extending her back

legs and positioning herself so that Klee could suckle. He tried to nurse on the hock of one leg but Artemisia shifted away from his awkward attempt until he found a teat.

As Artemisia nestled close to her baby, she felt content and in no hurry to get back to the small band of horses. She welcomed this time, free from Sargent's constant scrutiny and her duties as lead mare. With Mary, she had stayed away for a week, enjoying the solitude with her new foal, until they were discovered by Sargent and herded back to his harem.

Now, as the baby stood next to Artemisia and leaned his head against her neck, it was clear that his markings would be different from Sargent's, the golden palomino. As his hair dried and fluffed, Klee became a mirror of Artemisia: a tobiano Paint horse of brown-and-white puzzle pieces with a cloudlike mane and tail. Against the pending dawn, the light sections of their coats looked luminous and opalescent, but the dark of their bodies disappeared into the night. From a distance, mother and son became two fractured spirits drifting above the earth.

AGNES MENETTI, A PALLID VISION OF PROPERNESS, STOOD

in the doorway, tapped her cane, and commanded attention. At eighty-eight, her extraordinary posture, substantial chest, and smooth helmet of short white hair gave her the appearance of a giant pigeon. She had a faint white mustache and favored long stretchy skirts, ortho-pedic sandals, oversized white silk blouses, and always a beaded chain of pearls from which her eyeglasses dangled.

Maya often tried to imagine what Grandmother's life had been like before her father died. One of the house-keepers had told her that Grandmother had traveled and gone to luncheons and even volunteered, delivering meals to the ill and homebound. But Maya had never once seen her leave the property on Altadena Lane.

"Good evening, Grandmother," said Maya.

"Good evening, child." She inspected the table, nodded with satisfaction, and sat down. "Morgana, several leaves from the magnolia tree dropped this afternoon. The gardeners don't come for three more days. After dinner, pick them up and dispose of them. I cannot have foliage on the ground. It's unsightly and causes bacteria and mold. And I noticed several scratches on one of the patio chairs. . . ."

Maya rolled her eyes. The lawn furniture, garden pottery, walkways, yard statues, the exterior and interior of the house, and the great block wall that surrounded the side and back yards had been painted an eggshell white and were repainted at the first hint of wear. The van of a local painting contractor was almost a permanent fixture in the circular driveway. On Grandmother's whims, the workers descended with their equipment to cleanse everything of its brief history, leaving Maya's world on Altadena Lane the color of bleached sheets.

"Call Blanchard Painting," Grandmother continued. "They know me well and will be prompt. Have them come out tomorrow and give me an estimate on all of the outdoor furniture." She picked up a napkin, draped it across her lap, and turned to Maya. "School?"

A pleasant memory overtook Maya's common sense and she blurted, "Today Mrs. Webster turned off all the lights in the classroom and let us put our heads on our desks while . . ."

Grandmother's eyebrows arched upward. "I hope

this isn't something frivolous, Maya. I would hate to think that this school is like all the others."

Maya had changed schools eight times in six years and had learned to squelch any mention of friends, field trips, assemblies, or anything that might interfere with class time or homework. Otherwise, a new school would be on the horizon the next day. School would be out for the summer in a few weeks. Maya adored her teacher, and she had just discovered that Mrs. Webster would continue with the class into the next grade. Maya hoped to do the same.

Her mind searched for something other than the truth. "No, no. Nothing frivolous. Mrs. Webster was actually trying a new educational technique from an important teacher magazine to help us remember our spelling words by having us close our eyes and visualize them, like they do at the National Spelling Bee. She's very innovative and it was extremely effective. I got one hundred percent on my spelling test."

"I would expect nothing less. My Gregory, may he rest in peace, was always an excellent student. He never compromised his education, Maya, and you won't either." She looked at Morgana. "The meat?"

Morgana disappeared, reentered with the chuck roast on a serving platter, and placed it in the center of the table, exactly between the two side dishes of green beans and potatoes.

Maya's eyes scanned the eating surface for an offending drop of gravy. Grandmother had sent other housekeepers fleeing for as much, but unfortunately, Morgana had a steady hand.

Grandmother glanced down at the floor. "Morgana, did you mop and wax today?"

"Yes, Mrs. Menetti, not three hours ago."

Maya looked down at the white tile, which gleamed like an unwavering lake.

"I see a cloudy area," said Grandmother. "I cannot have inefficiency in this house, Morgana. Buff the floor after dinner."

Maya gave Morgana a pitying smile, as if to say, "See, she really is unreasonable."

Puzzled, Morgana said, "Certainly, Mrs. Menetti." She gave Maya a quick nod and a tight grimace and disappeared into the kitchen.

Maya ate with her eyes downcast. Not a word transpired. The air filled with the clink of silverware and Grandmother's sips and swallows. Sounds from the neighborhood beckoned through the open dining room window. One of the boys from across the street counted for a game of hide-and-seek. The ice-cream truck crawled down Altadena Lane with the tinkle of carnival music, followed by the squeals of children begging it to stop. Bike bells rang from the sidewalks. Maya gazed out but tried to look indifferent. Grandmother didn't believe in foolishness of any kind, ever.

Morgana walked into the dining room, wearing a look of smug superiority. "Mrs. Menetti, I hope I'm not presumptuous in presenting these to you, but you told me to be diligent in the supervision of Maya's time. I found her playing with these this afternoon. She keeps them hidden in her closet." She held out the shoe box.

Maya stood up, clutching her napkin. Her face pinched with disbelief. The pot roast jumbled in her stomach. "No!" she yelled.

Grandmother signaled for Morgana to come closer.

She lifted her eyeglasses to her face and looked inside. The photo of Maya's mother lay on top. "How long have these been in my house?"

For the first time, Maya could not think of a lie that would please Grandmother. "She . . . I . . . my . . . mother gave them to me when I was little. I didn't tell you . . ." Maya glanced at Morgana. "Because . . . you don't like horses."

Grandmother leaned forward, her eyes examining the girl. "Have you forgotten, Maya, that it was your mother's obsession with horses that was your parents' undoing?"

Maya sat down and stared into her plate.

Grandmother turned to the housekeeper. "You see, Morgana, my Gregory was well past the age to marry when he met Maya's mother. Over forty years old, successful in business, and firmly entrenched in Pasadena society. Then he went on a vacation to Wyoming. On a painting expedition, of all things, out in the wilderness. Oil painting was such a trivial, messy hobby. And then he met *that* woman. Imagine! She was half his age. Her family lived with animals. Like animals. He took her away from that desolate and forsaken place and brought her to civilization." Grandmother took a deep breath through her nose. "That's the kind of man he was, always wanting to help the less fortunate." Her eyes narrowed. "But she couldn't give up riding horses. And my son indulged her. They were on their way to one of those excursions in the middle of nowhere, so she could ride and he could paint, when the accident occurred." Her face lost expression and she seemed to retreat into her thoughts. "He was my only child, my sweet boy . . . and that woman and her horses took him away from me. She might as well have killed him with her own hand."

"My condolences, Mrs. Menetti," said Morgana. "So, with respect, ma'am, your son and daughter-in-law didn't die in a boating accident in Costa Rica?"

Grandmother snapped into the present. "Certainly not! Wherever did you get that idea?"

Morgana's eyes glared in Maya's direction.

Maya tried to look remorseful, but with each breath, her fury expanded like a balloon about to pop.

"My granddaughter has a vivid imagination, Morgana, but after all, she's only a child. She will outgrow it. My Gregory was truthful, and Maya will be just like him. Of that you can be certain. Put that box in the trash can in the alley. I will not have anything related to those filthy beasts or that woman in my house."

Morgana walked out with her head high and deliberate purpose in her steps.

The silence continued until Maya heard the back door click shut.

"Your Saturday library privilege is revoked," said Grandmother. "And you are excused to your bath."

Maya avoided Grandmother's eyes as she slid from her chair. She walked upstairs, her fists clenching and unclenching. She winced at the thought of losing her only weekly outing, one hour of precious library time supervised by the housekeeper. *The Big Book of Horse Facts* and *The Equine Encyclopedia* would have to wait, but it was just as well. She didn't want to go anywhere with Morgana anyway.

As Maya took her bath, her thoughts raced. The trash had been collected yesterday, on Thursday. Today was Friday. That left Maya one week to save her horses. As she dressed in her pajamas and robe, she comforted herself by recalling all the housekeepers she'd sabotaged in less time: Kathryn, by sneaking a blue sweatshirt into the washing machine with an all-white load of Grandmother's delicates; Patricia, by convincing her that Grandmother loved jalapeño peppers in her food; Laura, by assuring her that it wasn't inappropriate in the least to paint Maya's nails with bright red polish.

A wry smile crept onto Maya's face. One week was plenty of time.

5

Artemisia sensed she had been gone long enough.

She raised her muzzle, and her ears alerted and twitched. Something in the wind felt wrong. An innate urgency told her to return to the protection of her band. She left the birthing area with Klee in tow.

On the trail, if she shifted in one direction, Klee did the same, his spindly legs mimicking her movement. When he tried to stop to investigate a rock or a clump of greasewood, Artemisia nosed him to keep moving for fear he would become an easy meal for a hungry predator.

Artemisia led her obedient baby over the rise of a hill and was relieved to see the cluster of horses. She neighed, announcing their arrival. When all heads turned, she walked with slow and regal steps, proud to be bringing home the new addition and comforted by the safety of their numbers.

Sargent's alert head leaned in her direction, and he nickered as if to say, "You were missed. Welcome home. And who is this?" He did not rush to Artemisia. Instead, he stood aloof and on guard, keeping his vigilant post as protector.

Artemisia watched as Georgia came to say hello, making deep, soft nickers. She sniffed the baby with careful curiosity. Klee leaned his muzzle toward her and touched her nose but soon became shy and pulled back toward his mother. Wyeth approached with two-year-old boldness. When he seemed too forceful, Mary intervened and prevented his advances. Then she turned to nuzzle the foal. Artemisia allowed it. She already sensed Mary's protective nature toward her new brother.

Artemisia took a few steps away and peed a long stream.

Sargent marched over, sniffed the puddle, and covered it with his own stream, mixing their scents to make sure that any other males in the area knew that Artemisia belonged to him.

Artemisia ambled back to her foal and watched as Sargent came forward to meet his son, his huge body towering over the newborn. No one had taught Klee how to defer to the stallion, but he knew by instinct to pull back his lips and clap his teeth together as if telling his father, "I am young and small. I am not a threat to you. I need your guidance, so please don't hurt me." Satisfied with the appropriate submission, Sargent snuffled Klee's muzzle, then moved toward Artemisia. She felt the stallion's gentle tugs as he nibbled at her neck hair. She returned the favor and they quietly groomed each other.

Throughout the night, for several minutes every hour, Artemisia felt Klee sidle toward her, drawn to the safe smoothness of her underbelly and the milk. She welcomed him, adoring the closeness. Once he was nourished, she watched his every move until he folded to the ground with exhaustion. Even as he slept, Artemisia often dropped her head to his body, as if to reassure herself that he was safe and still breathing.

6

Maya took a deep breath, seething with resentment. She unlocked and opened the narrow French doors that led from her room to the balcony overlooking the side garden. Stepping onto the landing, she looked toward the far reaches of the backyard, knowing that her horses lay just beyond the great white block wall. How could she ever get them with Morgana and Grandmother on constant watch? And hadn't Grandmother always complained about transients who wandered in the alley and rummaged through the garbage? What if someone took the horses for their own children before Maya could reclaim them?

She turned back into her room, took the crisp, clean blouse that Morgana had readied for school tomorrow off the hanger, and returned to the balcony. She wadded the blouse into a tight ball, stepped on it, and mopped the deck.

As she stood in the almost dark, holding the now dirty and wrinkled blouse, the house next door began to illuminate as someone turned on lights, room by room. The people had just moved in and had not yet draped their windows. The upstairs bedroom opposite Maya's turned bright. A woman and a young girl entered. Maya felt riveted. The girl sat on the floor with a towel around her shoulders, and the woman sat behind her on the bed, combing out her tangled wet hair. The daughter chatted and the mother smiled. Even after the girl's hair looked sleek and straight, the mother kept combing, stroking, and listening.

Muffled voices broke Maya's reverie. Downstairs, Grandmother had begun her nightly inspection of the house to examine each room for hints of disorder. Morgana would follow, making notes on the housekeeper's clipboard for tomorrow's cleaning. Maya's bedroom was last on the schedule. She backed into her bedroom and shut and locked the French doors. She hung the blouse back on the hanger and crawled into bed, pretending to sleep.

Grandmother's and Morgana's voices became louder as they climbed the stairs. Doors opened and shut. Footsteps began and paused. Closer now, Grandmother's voice rose and fell with audible directives.

The bedroom door swung wide and the hall light flooded the room. Grandmother's cane tapped as she walked toward the closet.

Maya heard the closet light click on, and she waited for the discovery.

"Morgana! What is this? I asked you to wash and iron

Maya's blouse for school tomorrow. She cannot appear in public in that fashion. Do it tonight or I'll call the agency. . . ."

"But . . . I . . ." Morgana paused. "Yes, Mrs. Menetti." With clipped steps, Morgana walked toward the closet and then out of the room.

Under her blanket, Maya's face wrinkled with disappointment. Morgana had not even been flustered! After the door shut and Grandmother's footsteps subsided, Maya turned onto her back and stared at the honeycomb shadows on the ceiling. Tomorrow she would try another tactic. Maybe she could tell Grandmother that she'd overheard Morgana talking to the new neighbors next door about employment. That lie had worked one time before. Maya's thoughts drifted back to the woman and her daughter. What had the girl been telling her mother? she wondered.

If she had the chance, Maya knew exactly what she'd tell her own mother. She would tell her frivolous things. How Mrs. Webster had turned off all the lights in the classroom and let them rest their heads on their desks while she finished reading *King of the Wind* by Marguerite Henry, and how the entire class had clapped at the end of the story. And that Jeremiah Boswell had pushed a first grader and made him spill his lunch tray in the middle of the cafeteria. Jeremiah laughed so hard that he slipped and fell on the floor and his face landed smack in the creamed turkey and mashed potatoes. She would tell her mother about ice-cream trucks, bicycles, and foolishness of any kind.

Sunday afternoon, Maya squirmed on the plastic slipcover on the living room couch, trying not to slide off. At the same time, she struggled to hold a large photo album open on her lap.

Grandmother sat opposite her in a wingback chair, studying the estimate left by the painting contractor for the patio and lawn furniture. She flipped through a multitude of possible color samples.

Maya shook her head. Why did Grandmother even bother? She always chose the same color.

"Where are you now?" asked Grandmother.

"Tenth album. Fifth grade. Summer."

Every Sunday, Grandmother insisted they revisit several of the numbered albums that chronicled each year of her father's life.

"Yes, that was . . ."

Maya whispered "Big Bear Lake" in unison with Grandmother. She could recite the events by heart. In third grade he had fallen from his bicycle and had broken his arm. He received a trumpet for his eleventh birthday. In high school he was on the chess and tennis teams. He collected stamps, was allergic to cats, and loved to travel by train. He had wanted to be an artist, but Grandmother had discouraged his folly in favor of a respectable job in accounting instead. She didn't mind if he dabbled in art because, until he went to Wyoming and started painting horses, it had been simply harmless recreation. Maya had never seen any of his paintings and never would. Grandmother had destroyed all the painful reminders of that "unfortunate time."

Maya replaced the album in the long cupboard and removed another, farther down the row. She took it to the couch, opened it, and came across a photo in which Grandmother had clipped out her mother's image, leaving Maya intact, floating in the middle of the picture, as if no one had been holding her. A familiar anger bit her like a tick. Maya traced around the edge of the picture now in the shape of a puzzle piece, showing only a portion of her mother's hand and a wisp of her hair. The desire for revenge engorged. She knew that the one connection to her mother had also been cut from her life and was now in the trash.

"Maya, you look flushed," said Grandmother. "You'll stay home from school tomorrow until your color improves."

Maya shook her head and pleaded, "No. I feel fine!" She sometimes had to miss school for weeks because of

Grandmother's random and bizarre notions that she might be getting sick.

"Nevertheless. It's safer here."

Maya crossed her arms on her chest and glowered at Grandmother, knowing there would be no use in arguing. She couldn't go to school. She couldn't go to the library. Her horses were in the trash along with the only picture of her mother. *A journey about to begin?* That was ridiculous. She wasn't going anywhere.

Maya continued to stare at Grandmother, who pretended to be concerned with the paint samples. Suddenly, Maya not only wanted to get rid of Morgana, but she felt an overwhelming desire to punish Grandmother, too.

Grandmother found the color she wanted and wrote her decision on the clipboard. "There. I'll tell Morgana to call first thing in the morning and to have the painters come on Tuesday." She excused herself and left the clipboard and pen on the coffee table.

Maya stared at the clipboard. She leaned forward and twisted her head in order to read Grandmother's writing.

Call Blanchard Painters. Color Number 34.

Maya's eyes darted around the room. She listened for footsteps. Hearing none, she flipped through the samples and found number 34, the inevitable eggshell white, then continued until she found another. She picked up the pen. With quick and careful precision, she made a teensy adjustment to Grandmother's writing. It now said:

Call Blanchard Painters. Color Number 84.

Satisfied, Maya stood and walked from the room, pausing every few steps. With deliberate fervor, she dragged the edge of her shoe across the immaculate tile, leaving long black scuff marks.

On Tuesday, when Grandmother woke from her nap, she called Maya to her bedroom. "Come here, child, and look out this window. I seem to be having trouble with my vision." She removed her glasses, cleaned them, repositioned the lenses on her face, then squinted as she looked through the pane and into the backyard. "It must be an odd reflection of the sun. Do you see it, too?"

Maya peered into the backyard and bit her lip to contain her smile. "I see the painters, Grandmother. And the furniture you wanted painted. But . . . didn't you tell Morgana that you wanted the furniture to be white?"

Grandmother blinked hard and leaned closer to the window. She stared bug-eyed at the yard. Her lips trembled. She grabbed her cane and stormed down-stairs, through the house, and into the yard, huffing like a locomotive.

Maya followed, skipping.

The bewildered painters displayed their work order.

Three tables, twelve chairs, four lawn chaises, and any number of assorted plant stands had been sprayed a stunning pink, which closely resembled the color of liquid stomach medication. It now looked as if a flock of giant and garish wrought-iron flamingos had landed on the lawn in a circus of contortions.

Within the hour, Morgana had been relieved of her duties and another housekeeper had been enlisted from the agency. She would arrive tomorrow. After the trauma of the afternoon, Grandmother retired to her bedroom and reclined. While she recuperated with a cool towel on her forehead, Maya raced to the backyard.

She opened the large wooden gate in the white block wall, stepped into the alley, and lifted the lid of the trash can. Smells accosted her: citrus from the recently pruned orange tree, soured garbage, and fermented grass cuttings. She pillaged beneath a pile of newspapers until she spied the box. Although the cardboard was a bit damp from chamomile tea bags, the horses and the photo of her mother had stayed dry and clean.

Maya hugged the shoe box to her chest. "I will keep you safe," she whispered. "I promise."

Insistent whispers invaded Maya's early morning dreams. "Maya, wake up!"

She squinted through half sleep.

Valentina, the new employee, hovered above her. Her forehead crinkled and her brown eyes pleaded with desperation. "I need help. Your grandmother . . . she is very unusual this morning . . . very confused about many little things. Nothing I am doing is right, but I am doing everything the same. I took her morning tea on the tray, but she is calling me a different name, Monica, and she says I am to cook my special eggs, Eggs Monica? I do not know what is Eggs Monica."

Perplexed, Maya sat up. Although Valentina had only been with them for a few days, Grandmother had never mistaken one housekeeper for another. She searched her memory for someone named Monica and remembered. "She worked here two years ago and made scrambled eggs with cream . . . and, I think, cheddar cheese."

Valentina rubbed her face with both hands. She looked much too weary for so early in the morning.

Maya had seen that look before and felt sorry for Valentina. She seemed nice but the nice ones always collapsed the easiest. "I'll show you. The recipes are in a little box." Maya flung off her covers and quickly dressed.

In the kitchen, Maya read the instructions as Valentina cooked the eggs, and then coached her on the position of the mandatory two pieces of toast on the plate, cut diagonally.

Maya looked at the clock and eased into the dining room. Grandmother's place was already set with a saucer displaying half of a grapefruit with a cherry eye.

Grandmother appeared in the doorway and tapped her cane.

"Good morning, Grandmother," said Maya.

The woman nodded. She seemed to teeter over her cane and took longer than usual to reach her chair.

Valentina entered and set Grandmother's plate in front of her.

Grandmother picked up her fork, stabbed a bite of the eggs, and put them in her mouth. She squinted and coughed. "Too much pepper!"

Confused, Valentina stammered, "There . . . is . . . no . . . pepper."

Grandmother slapped the table. "I will not have an employee who lies to me. I hope I don't have to call the agency. . . ."

"She's not lying!" said Maya. "I watched her. She didn't use any pepper."

Grandmother's face reddened. It was as if something

swelled inside her, about to explode. There was a second of doomed silence, and then it happened so fast that Maya only glimpsed a blur hurtling through the air.

The china plate hit the wall and clattered to the floor, breaking into precise thirds, in perfect triangular pieces. Yellow lumps of egg left more than one excuse to call in the painters. Puzzled, Maya stared at the shards and wondered how Grandmother had shattered the plate with such symmetry.

Maya turned to see Grandmother's head falling forward and hitting the table with a dull thump.

Valentina put both of her hands over her mouth.

Maya sat transfixed and stared at Grandmother, who slumped over her breakfast. Her face rested on a pillow of grapefruit, its juice dribbling onto the tablecloth.

Valentina ran to the kitchen and Maya could hear her

frantic voice on the telephone, giving the address and telling someone to hurry.

Then, as if someone had pinched her, Maya's mind leaped to the possibility that Grandmother might not wake up. She ran to her and put both hands on her fallen shoulders. "Grandmother? Grandmother?"

Grandmother's body drooped and her arms dangled at her sides, like weighted lines.

Valentina appeared and gently pulled Maya away. "Help is coming. They are on the way."

"What's wrong with her? Why isn't she moving?"

Valentina wrung her hands. "I do not know. She needs a doctor."

Confusion and hysteria welled inside Maya. She yelled, "Grandmother! Wake up! Wake up right now!"

In the distance, the whine of an ambulance escalated.

7

ARTEMISIA SAW THE BLEACHED BONES OF A HORSE SKELE-
ton lying in a deep gully. She led the band away from the ledge
and the tenuous footing and the consequences of what could happen if one of the horses fell, broke a leg, and couldn't get up.

Artemisia was the lead mare and even though she had a
new foal who needed to nurse for several minutes every hour, the
survival and well-being of the entire group also rested on her.
She determined where and when to stop and graze. The others
followed. If they were pursued, she didn't panic or lead them
into dead-end canyons where they might be trapped. She led
them to safety. And to the places they would rest each evening. And to water. Now, she stopped and looked toward the
watering hole with alert caution, aware that another band
was drinking there. The stallion in that band was aggressive

and liked to fight. Artemisia would hold her band back until they left.

When it was their turn, she led them forward. Klee dawdled, listing a little too far from the cluster. Georgia gave him a firm head shove to keep him in line.

Sargent patrolled from behind, keeping all of them in his sights. When they stopped at the water's edge, he approached each mare and nickered, taking attendance. Then, after drinking almost a gallon of water, Sargent raised his head to inspect the area before allowing the others to satisfy their thirst.

Klee frolicked. He ran around Artemisia in ever-widening circles as if she were a maypole and there was a tether between them. He took short jaunts away, high stepping and kicking out with his hind legs, already imitating his brother and father, but then rushed back to the security of his mother. He ran to Mary and nibbled a little too roughly at her neck. She shook him off.

The excited foal turned his attention to Wyeth, who sent him tumbling with a playful kick. Klee pranced up to Sargent and pestered him to engage in a bout of rambunctious play. Artemisia pushed herself between the father and son to dissuade Klee, but the eager baby darted around her, bucking at the big stallion's back legs. Sargent whinnied and nipped at him. Artemisia saw that Sargent was preoccupied with standing guard. She intervened again, positioning herself between Klee and the others. Over and over the colt tried to reenter the circle, but Artemisia moved as he moved, blocking his advances toward the band.

Klee soon became anxious. He hung his head and approached Artemisia with penitent baby steps. When he leaned in to nibble her neck, she relented, and permitted him back into their small community.

Maya wondered for the thousandth time if her new family would welcome her. She straightened her plaid skirt from beneath the scrunch of the airplane seat belt, brushed lint from her white blouse and blue cardigan, and looked out the window of the airplane at the strange landscape below. The pilot had announced that they were flying over Nevada and into Utah, but there were no towns that she could see, only barren brown flatlands, dry lake beds, and the occasional canyon that dropped into the muddled unknown.

The plane had reached its cruising altitude and seemed to float. Maya wondered at the peculiarity of time. It seemed as if hours slowed from this vantage. Maybe that's what happened, she thought. Seconds and minutes had elongated, making room for the crush of events that changed her life. Since the moment Grandmother had tasted imaginary pepper in her scrambled eggs, Maya felt as if she had lived months instead of only the last twenty-four hours.

She closed her eyes but could not escape yesterday's unforgettable images: Grandmother's body disappearing on a rolling bed into a white ambulance; the doctor in the white lab coat who delivered the unbelievable news; Grandmother's lawyer, Mr. Benedetto, rushing to meet them at the hospital, still in his tennis clothes after being called off the courts; and later, the incongruity of walking back across the threshold of the house on Altadena Lane without Grandmother.

It had been late afternoon when Mr. Benedetto escorted Maya to the couch in the living room. Maya had always liked his shiny bald head with the smile of curly gray hair around the back and the way his eyeglasses perched so far on the end of his nose that they looked as if they might fall off. He sat in the wingback chair across from her and leaned forward with sincere interest. "Maya, I'm very sorry about your grandmother. It was a massive stroke. According to her wishes, there will be no service. And I'll take care of all the other arrangements. You should know that there's a trust for your college education, but we don't have to talk about that until a much later date. The house and the furniture have been left to the Historic Pasadena Heritage League. They'll use it for functions . . . weddings and such. All of the personal and small household items will be put in storage for you, for some day when you're ready for them. Right now, we need to be concerned about your

care. I've asked the housekeeper to stay with you overnight until I can make arrangements. It looks as if you'll
have to leave a little early for Wyoming this year."

"Wyoming?"

"Well, yes . . ." said Mr. Benedetto. "To the
Limners, like you do every year. But of course this
time . . . to stay for good."

Confused, Maya asked, "Who are they?"

"Who are they?" Mr. Benedetto almost laughed. "Your
mother's family. You spend every summer with them."

She stared at him, her eyes vacant and bewildered.

Mr. Benedetto's brow furrowed and he sat straighter,
flipping through a sheaf of papers. He pointed to a para-
graph. "Those were your parents' wishes. It says that
your custody was to be split. You were to spend the
school year with your grandmother and your summers

with . . ." He read the paper. "'Walter, Frederick, and Violet Limner.'" He looked up and raised his eyebrows as if asking a question.

Maya gave a tiny shrug.

With sudden revelation, Mr. Benedetto rolled his eyes toward the ceiling and leaned back in his chair. "Oh, Agnes," he said, as if he were admonishing Grandmother. "So that's why she never had me to the house during the summer. She didn't want me to find out that she wasn't complying." He took a deep breath. "Maya, do you know *anything* about your mother's family?"

Maya searched her memory for the details Grand-mother had told her and slowly nodded. "My other grandmother died when my mother was really little. I have a grandfather and he lives with his brother and sister . . . but they're actually hillbillies with no education and they live like pigs in an uncivilized land. Oh, and they don't appreciate culture and are extremely crass and unsavory."

Mr. Benedetto smiled and shook his head. "Maya, I think that's a gross misconception on Agnes's part." He studied the papers. "Here's the information for Walter Limner. I'll call as soon as I get back to the office, then I'll call Valentina with the details for your flight. I'll see you tomorrow. And please, don't worry." He stood and left, shaking his head and muttering to himself.

Alone in the room, Maya couldn't help but worry. She was curious about her mother's family and kept rolling their names around in her mind: Walter, Frederick, and Violet. They sounded like nice names. But what if

Grandmother had been right about them? Or knew something much worse than what she'd told Maya? After all, she'd kept her from them for all these years. And why hadn't *they* tried to contact her? Hadn't they wanted her? For all she knew they could be mean and indifferent. But then, what difference would it make if they were? She had nowhere else to go.

Valentina helped Maya pack. Everything she owned fit into one small suitcase. Afterward, Maya walked downstairs, stopping on each step in front of her father's photographs to touch his face. She wandered from room to room, her footsteps echoing hollow good-byes. When she heard children playing outside, she realized that she could walk out the front door and join them. But she didn't. She meandered inside without direction, studying the furniture stifled beneath the plastic slipcovers, stroking the stark walls, and slipping behind the white draperies that dared not rumple. She walked into the dining room and gingerly touched each of the milk-glass vases for the first time in her life. As she climbed the stairs to go to bed, she thought about the voluminous white wedding gowns and the trailing white veils that would someday sweep across the immaculate tile floors. Grandmother would have liked that.

When the airplane's wheels finally touched down and the brakes engaged, Maya leaned against the seat, clutching the box of horses. She waited until everyone was off the plane and then edged down the aisle toward the waiting flight attendant.

As they walked down the long jet-way tunnel, he turned and smiled. "Visiting or going home?"

Maya's forehead crinkled as she thought about the question. She raised and dropped her shoulders. "I don't know."

Jog

MAYA OPENED THE SHOE BOX AND PULLED OUT THE
brown-and-white horse, turning it over and over in her
hand. She sat up straight and expectant in the hard plastic chair next to the airline counter in Salt Lake City, but
her stomach wobbled. There was so much she did not
know. Dinnertime, for instance, and how often her
grandfather would inspect her closet and what the consequences might be for smudged shoes. She gripped the
plastic horse tighter in her fist. The terminal had thinned
of people. She stared at each man who walked by and
wondered which one might be him. It occurred to her
that he might not come at all. Then what would she do?

Through the panorama of windows, Maya saw a
tall, burly man with sandy-brown hair salted with gray

walking toward the terminal. He wore a cowboy hat, sunglasses, and a blue work shirt. Mud crusted his boots. A shiny buckle adorned a leather belt. A small lilting recognition ran through Maya's body. But why? she wondered. Had she met him before? The automatic doors parted. With a long stride, he hurried to the counter. He glanced at Maya but spoke with the clerk, showing his identification and signing a paper. Then he moved toward her.

She tilted her chin upward to view all of his height.

A voice that sounded as if it came from a deep barrel said, "Hello, Maya."

Maya swallowed hard. If this giant had the inclination, he could hurt her with a flick of his bowl-sized hand.

He reached out and put tentative fingers on her head.

Maya leaned away.

He took off his sunglasses, pulled a handkerchief from his pants pocket, and blotted at his teary eyes. His sniffling got louder. Maya had never seen a man weep before. Wasn't he embarrassed to be crying in front of a complete stranger? She stared at the floor.

"I'm 'Moose' Limner. Walter, your grandfather." His eyes filled again and he choked out the words. "I'm sorry for this display. But . . . seeing you after all these years, well, it's quite a shock. You look so much like your mother, sitting there like a little bird. I used to call her that, you know. Ellie-bird."

"Ellie," Maya repeated. She couldn't remember the last time she'd heard her mother's name. A long-forgotten memory made Maya feel tense with trepidation. In an instant, she was six years old again, in Grandmother's backyard, skipping and weaving between the white lawn furniture with a pinwheel in her hand. The star spun in the breeze, and she had mindlessly repeated her mother's first name to the tune of "Twinkle, Twinkle, Little Star." Grandmother had overheard the singing, washed Maya's mouth out with soap, and threw the toy in the trash.

Moose gave his nose a healthy blow into the handkerchief and then stuffed it back into his pocket. "Well now, enough of my blubbering. Let's get you home." He held out his hand.

Maya stood, feeling like a small sapling next to a giant oak, but didn't reach out to him.

He finally dropped his arm to his side. "The truck is parked in the lot." He picked up her suitcase and turned away.

Maya followed. She climbed into the cab on the

passenger side. A pillow and a folded quilt occupied the middle of the seat. Maya stayed as close to the passenger door as possible and held the box of horses on her lap, except for the brown-and-white Paint that she still clutched.

"These early June evenings can be chilly. The blanket and pillow are for you. And in that bag on the floor is a sandwich your uncle Fig made. We're headed about four hours northeast into Wyoming, so we wanted you to be comfortable."

Maya nodded. They were soon away from the traffic of the city and on a highway, weaving upward through grass foothills. Her eyes darted from the windshield to the side window, trying to absorb the new world. The terrain became dry and gave way to red rock mountains.

Ominous cliffs, like the chiseled faces of train engines, jutted toward them. The sun dipped and the colors of the jagged landscape intensified as if a paintbrush had streaked the hills with a rust wash.

"Pretty, isn't it?" said Moose.

"I guess," said Maya, thinking of the lush and colorful Altadena Lane.

Moose nodded toward her hand. "I notice you still have your mother's horses."

"Yes, sir," she said. Maya quickly slipped the small horse into the box.

"I wasn't going to take it from you," said Moose. "And Maya, I've been waiting a long time to see you again, and I wasn't planning on you calling me 'sir.' But you can call me 'Moose' if it makes you feel more comfortable. Everyone else does. 'Course I would love it if you called me 'Grandpa' again, when you're ready. You don't remember, but you had just turned four the last time your mother brought you home for a visit. That's when she found those horses in her closet and gave them to you. She was planning on bringing you back but . . ." Moose's voice cracked. He began sniffling again, then cleared his throat and changed the subject. "See those mountains in the distance? Those are the Wind River Mountains, the continuation of the great Rockies. Locals call them 'The Winds.'" He pointed northeast. "That's the direction we're heading, straight for the prow of The Winds. It might not seem like it, but we're pretty high up in elevation. We'll be at a little over seven thousand feet when we get to the ranch."

Maya looked toward the horizon at the jury of mountain peaks far in the distance. In between, nothing interrupted the expanse of desert except the highway and the long scars of snow fences. The air chilled. The sky darkened. Maya pulled the quilt to her lap and spread it over her legs and the box of horses, as much for protection from the unfamiliar as for warmth.

"Do you remember the ranch?" asked Moose.

The ranch. The word triggered vague feather-light images. "I don't think so," said Maya.

"Well, maybe you will when you see it."

An oncoming car's high beams illuminated the cab, barraging them with bright light. Moose blinked the truck lights, and the other driver dimmed the blinding rays. Traffic waned, and soon they were a solitary truck heading to somewhere. A weariness spread over Maya and she slumped toward the pillow. The cab was dark and the motor thrummed. Her eyes closed, but before falling asleep, a minuscule excitement, like a seedling poking through spring ground, wiggled in her mind.

10

Maya heard the unmistakable sound of a whimpering animal and startled awake. Was it a dream? What
time was it? If she were late for breakfast, Grandmother
would be furious. Even more distressing was the discovery that she'd slept in yesterday's clothes. With a quick
jerk, she sat up, whipping her head to scan the strange
room. Like sporadic raindrops, the events of the last two
days settled in her consciousness. She took a deep breath
and studied her surroundings.

A paneled ceiling sloped downward and met two
dormer windows that allowed streams of sunlight to
puddle on the floor. She sat in a bed with an old-fashioned
iron headboard and footboard. Her box of horses had
been placed on a knotty pine dresser and her suitcase

propped open the door leading to a long hallway of hardwood.

The whining started again, louder now. Something *was* in the room!

A short-haired brown dog leaped from the floor onto the end of the bed and crawled close to her, its tail thumping the covers. Maya screamed and pulled the blanket over her head.

Footsteps pounded down the hall.

"Golly, get down!" a man's voice called. Maya heard a thud and nails clicking on the floor.

"You can come out now," said the voice.

Maya lowered the blanket to see a man who was as tall as Moose, but so thin she wondered how he kept his pants up. His nose would have been too big for his face had a well-trimmed beard not balanced it out. The purple-blue eyes and reddish hair guaranteed his relation to Maya. A dish towel hung from his waist, a cooking fork sprouted from one hand, and he smelled like bacon.

"I'm your great-uncle Fig," he announced. "I'm Moose's older brother, which makes me the boss, at least in my mind. My real name is Frederick, but you can imagine why I prefer Fig. And you're Maya."

The dog appeared again, braced its paws against the side of the bed, and strained upward, panting.

"This is my dog, Golly. She's dying for you to pet her."

Maya pulled back. "Dogs are mean and dirty and they bite children."

"What? Where did you hear that?" asked Fig. "And anyway, not Golly. She's a sweetheart, and I just gave her a bath myself yesterday. Come on. Give her a pat on the head. I'm warning you, though. Once you start, she'll drive you crazy wanting more."

"Grandmother said . . . said they carry dander and they're unsanitary . . . for my lungs. I . . . might actually be allergic."

Uncle Fig looked skeptical. "I hope not, because Golly's not leaving anytime soon. Best give her a wide berth."

Uncle Fig started for the door.

The dog stared at Maya, then tilted her head and lifted her ears.

"But what if she jumps on me or something? I could catch rabies or fleas or ticks."

By now, Fig was in the hall. "She might lick you to

death but that's about it. She's had all of her shots, so all you'll catch from Golly is her good nature."

"Wait! Where's my . . . where's Moose?" she called.

Fig clamored down the stairs and hollered, "He's in the kitchen. If you get up, I'll fix you some pancakes. The b-a-c-o-n is ready, but we'd better get to it before Golly figures out what I'm spelling."

As if the dog understood, she dashed from the room.

Maya slid out of bed and peeked down the hallway to make sure they were gone. She retrieved the box of horses from the dresser and climbed onto the seat beneath one of the dormer windows.

Staring out, she sucked in her breath. It looked like a picture from a library book: A tidy grass apron wrapped around the house. Scarlet honeysuckle crawled on the split-rail fence that bordered a long graveled drive. A procession of mountains framed the horizon. She saw rows of corrals and an even larger pasture defined by wooden fences. But the corrals and pasture were empty. Where were the horses?

Maya glanced back into the room. The position of the bed, the light on the floor, the sloped ceiling, and the window seat where she now sat felt familiar. Maya froze and shivers ran up her arms.

This was the very spot in which she had once played with her mother.

As she ran her fingers over the faded calico fabric on the bench seat, blue with tiny comets, she whispered, "Running free and belonging only to the stars." Maya opened the shoe box, and with deliberate care, placed the brown-and-white Paint on the narrow sill with her mother's photo, facing out.

"Maya, the pancakes are ready," called Uncle Fig from the bottom of the stairs. "And Golly is staring at your b-a-c-o-n!"

Maya looked at the unmade bed. What would be the punishment for not making it before breakfast? The wafting smell of bacon and pancakes called to her stomach but she couldn't take a chance. She pulled the blankets from the bed, which was much bigger than her twin in Pasadena.

Uncle Fig found her struggling with the heavy top quilt. He stood in the doorway with a hand on one hip. In the other hand, he held a pair of small boots.

Maya jumped when she saw him.

"Didn't mean to scare you," said Fig, setting the boots on the floor. "Here. Let me help you with that." He took the big quilt and fluffed it over the bed and lined up the pillows. "You know, I've spent a fair part of my life studying the art of being messy. If you keep up all this fussiness, it's going to make me look bad. Understand?"

She nodded.

"Don't look so serious. I'm teasing and you're not in trouble. Now, hurry and change your clothes. Wear some long pants if you have any, and those are some old boots of your mother's that we never could part with. They look the right size but wear two pairs of socks if they're too big. We need to get some food in your stomach. I can hear it growling. You're not allergic to pancakes, are you?"

Maya shook her head.

Before he walked out the door, he turned to Maya, who was still standing stock-still, and winked at her. "You're a skinny thing," he said. "You must take after me."

Maya's face relaxed and a small smile escaped.

She dressed and pulled on the boots, which fit perfectly, and stroked the worn leather calves. She was glad they weren't new. Glad the boots carried all of her mother's experiences. She wished that she could soak all of their history from the scuffed toes all the way up into her head. She stood. They made her taller, but she felt awkward and unsure of her new stance. As she walked down the hall, she held on to the oak banister. White paint had worn off and bare wood showed through in streaks. Had her mother worn off the paint from years of walking down these stairs? Slowly, she descended the steps, massaging the smooth wood.

The stairs turned and deposited her into the living room. A large painting of a black stallion with a white blaze and white stockings hung on the main wall, centered above the sofa. Maya stepped closer, captivated by the sweeping ebony brushstrokes of the mane, the arched neck, and the defiance in the horse's posture. She leaned forward, her eyes following the thick, sculpted swirls of the oil paints. She took a deep breath, already loving this place, and turned to look at the rest of the room.

Knickknacks crowded the end tables and threatened to topple at the slightest nudge. The furniture looked worn but comfortable. The wood floors had yellowed with aged varnish. A corner fireplace made from river stones angled across two walls and was crowned with a dark soot halo. On either side of the hearth, the walls held a hodgepodge of photos of her mother on horseback, holding up prizes for one competition or another: ribbons, fancy belt buckles, and trophies. In one of the photos, a younger Golly sat at her mother's feet. Maya picked up a framed photo from a table. Her mother held a four-year-old Maya in her arms and a boy about the same age. Who was he?

As Maya's eyes flitted from picture to picture, she heard Moose's voice in the next room and tiptoed out of the living room and closer to the kitchen door to eavesdrop.

"I just can't forget what the lawyer told us. She *should* have been coming here regular, every summer. That old hen lied to us. 'No arrangements for visitation.' Those were her exact words every time I called. I should have never believed her!"

"No need to speak ill of the dead," said Fig. "You had

no reason not to believe her. She hoodwinked us, plain and simple. At least we finally know that Ellie and Greg wanted Maya to spend time with us. It's just too bad it was so long in coming."

"It breaks my heart to have to get rid of her so soon after we just got her back," said Moose.

Maya's brow puckered. Get rid of her? She pushed through the swinging door into the sunny kitchen with its faded blue linoleum and yellow cupboards, which needed repainting. Suds and dishes filled one side of the sink, and fresh grease spots peppered the white enameled stove. Moose sat at one end of a long trestle table on a bench seat, sipping coffee.

She stood in the center of the room and folded her arms across her chest. "You're getting rid of me . . . ?"

Fig and Moose exchanged glances.

"Now, that isn't exactly true or by choice," began Moose.

"Sit down and let us explain," said Fig, herding Maya to a seat at the table. "You see, Moose and I are taking you to the Sweetwater River to stay with your great-aunt Violet. She's our baby sister. But I'm warning you, no one has dared call her Violet in years, except behind her back. We call her Vi, rhymes with pie."

"Maya, the camp is nature at its finest," said Moose. "You'll sleep in a tepee, live around a campfire, and ride a horse every day. In fact, you'll see more horses in a summer than most people see in a lifetime. And we'll be out there soon enough."

"See, we're all here together in the house for most of the year," said Fig. "Even your aunt Vi. During school months, she teaches classes at the college. Art history, painters of the American Southwest, that sort of thing. Moose and I hire out in town. He's a farrier, shoeing horses, and I'm a handyman. Being as smart as I am, I can do almost anything."

"Which means he's a master of nothing," said Moose.

Uncle Fig pointed his spatula at Moose. "I'm warning you. Don't rile the cook."

Moose ignored him. "In the summer, Aunt Vi sets up a field camp. She writes articles for horse magazines and some years she takes groups out to photograph or paint scenes of the wilderness and the wild horses. . . ."

"Like my father did?"

"That's right," said Fig. "That's how he met Ellie way back when. Your father signed up for a week-long trip, and Aunt Vi outfitted the group. She provided the folks with tepees, food, and horses, and was their guide on top of it all. That's one of your father's paintings in the living room."

Her father had painted that beautiful stallion? A small satisfied smile appeared on Maya's face. A piece of her father was in this house, too. At least one painting had escaped Grandmother's wrath.

Moose cleared his throat. "In a few weeks, our business will slow down for the summer and we'll come out to camp. But first, Fig and I need to finish our work obligations near the ranch. We weren't expecting you, Maya. But we're sure glad you're here."

"Your cousin, Payton, is already out there with Vi," said Fig.

Maya's eyes brightened. "A girl?"

"No," said Fig. "And for your sake, I'm sorry that he's not. Payton is my ten-year-old grandson. See, some years back, my son married a nice widow-lady who already had three boys. Then Payton came along. Don't get me wrong. We love them all, but his older brothers have taught him every bit of mischief known to man and on top of that he's wound tight. He comes here every summer from their ranch in Colorado to spend time with our side of the family. And to give his parents a little breather."

Maya groaned. Would he be like the two brothers across the street on Altadena Lane who had seemed interested only in wrestling on their front lawn, frying leaves with a magnifying glass, and spitting in the gutter? Besides, Maya wasn't ready to leave this house. She wanted to soak up all the little details of her mother's life. She wanted to sit and gaze at her father's painting for a very long time. What could she say to convince them to let her stay?

"Oh, that's okay. You don't have to take me there just yet." She tried to keep her voice light and matter-of-fact. "I'll wait for you. You can work during the day and I'll stay right here. I won't put a toe outside. I'm absolutely used to that and I can be extremely helpful. I actually did all the housework at Grandmother's: cleaning, laundry, floors, even cooking. I could scrub those cupboards and I could even clean the hearth in the other room. It's positively filthy and I can reach it easily with a stepstool. Then we can all go out to . . . the frontier . . . together."

"Whoa! Sit down and eat your breakfast," said Uncle Fig, putting a plate in front of Maya and tapping her on the head with a pot holder. "I'm the chief cook and bottle washer around here."

"We can't just leave you alone all day," said Moose.

95

"Not in good conscience. And your aunt Vi has her heart set on spending this time with you."

Maya looked from Moose to Fig, trying to think of a more persuasive story. She put her elbows on the table and rested her chin in her hands, secretly pinching her cheeks and trying to make them look red. Maybe they would let her stay inside until her color improved. With wide and sincere eyes, Maya said, "I don't think it would be prudent to take me there just yet . . . with my condition."

Moose and Fig exchanged a curious glance.

"Your condition?" asked Moose.

"Yes. I have . . . that sickness people get from being high up in the mountains. You told me last night that we're at *seven thousand* feet."

"Altitude sickness?" said Fig. "Do you have a

headache? Are you feeling dizzy? Better drink lots of water."

"Yes! Altitude sickness. And I did feel dizzy when I first got up. I'm from Pasadena, which is practically near the ocean and that's sea level. Now that I'm here, I actually already feel like I'm going to get an excruciating headache. And maybe a fever." She put the back of her hand across her forehead for effect. "I get the sickness every time I go to the mountains. Grandmother took me skiing every February in California at Snow Summit and I always caught it. I couldn't leave the area until it cleared up completely, which usually took about . . . at least two weeks."

Fig put a pot holder over his mouth and turned back to the stove.

Moose massaged his chin with a thumb and forefinger,

mulling over what Maya had said. "Well now, that does present a problem. But Aunt Vi would be very disappointed if we don't show up with you this afternoon, and we try not to cross her if it can be helped. And you know, Maya, your mother spent every one of her growing-up summers at the camp with Vi. We're fairly certain that's why your mother wanted you to spend your summers here, too . . . so you could have the same experience. We're not about to go against your parents' wishes, especially since your grandmother did that for too many years." Moose's eyes watered and he mopped them with a napkin. "I hope you understand."

Maya had never seen a man who wept as easily and it made her feel uncomfortable and a bit jealous. Her shoulders drooped and she nodded with resignation. "I don't even know how to ride a horse."

"Aunt Vi will teach you to ride in no time," said Fig. "Just like she taught your mother and Payton. The Limners were born to ride. There's not one of us who didn't take to the saddle. Aunt Vi's a bit stubborn and has to have everything her way, but she's the finest horsewoman in the county. We've already trailered the horses to the camp for the summer. You'll be riding Seltzer."

"Seltzer?"

"A beautiful blue roan," said Moose. "Aunt Vi has taken him out on any number of journeys and he's sweet and dependable."

Maya studied the blueberries in her pancakes. Her mind became a mash of thoughts: a stubborn great-aunt Violet who two grown men didn't want to cross, a cousin who'd been taught all the mischief known to man, a wilderness where she might disappear and never be seen or heard from again, and the very animals that were her parents' undoing. And that one word that had fastened itself to her heart. *Journeys.* As she pushed the bacon around on her plate, her body pulsed with a combination of dread and excitement.

"Better eat up," said Fig, "Then head upstairs and collect your things. We're going to have to load the truck right after breakfast and get on the road."

After she finished eating, Maya left Moose and Fig with their coffee. She pushed through the swinging door and, as it closed behind her, she paused on the other side to listen.

"I'm trying to imagine those three out there together," said Fig. "My, oh my. Vi and Payton may have met their match."

Moose chuckled. "Or Maya will meet hers."

11

Maya sat sandwiched in the truck cab between Moose and Fig with her box of horses on her lap. Golly sat in Fig's lap, hanging her head out the truck window. Sprinkles of dog fur floated through the air, and occasionally a bit of slobber hit the wind and came back in Maya's face. She coughed and sputtered and rubbed at her cheeks, but neither Moose nor Fig seemed concerned about her possible dog allergy.

They had been driving on the high desert plain for almost two hours. Uncle Fig narrated like a tour guide, pointing out a llama farm, an actual moose by a stream, several herds of mule deer, and a bald eagle. "See that yellow-blooming bush on your left? That's rabbitbrush, *Chrysothamnus nauseosus*. The *nauseosus* part refers to its foul taste. Know what we have right here in Wyoming that's special to the American West? *Antilocapra americana,* the pronghorn. Looks sort of like a deer and sort of like a goat. Of course a lot of what we have here is one variety or another of sagebrush like *Artemisia tridentata.*" Uncle Fig's arm swept across the cab to indicate the vast gray-green ocean that reached both horizons. "Notice how your grandpa is keeping quiet? That's because he can't remember a Latin name from his own."

"Now, that's not true. I'm just letting your uncle Fig show off. I couldn't get a word in edgewise even if I wanted to, since he goes on and on and on. Someone in the family has to be the strong silent type and someone has to be the blabbermouth."

Maya's head turned from one man to the other. Sitting between Moose and Fig was like trying to follow a ball at a Ping-Pong match, so easily did they tease back and forth.

"I know the Latin name for bison," said Moose. "Want to hear it, Maya?"

She nodded.

"*Bison bison.*"

Fig slapped his leg. "That's the *only* one he can remember."

Maya bit back a smile.

"We've got a lot of exotic things out here, Maya," said Fig. "Just pay attention and you'll get an eyeful."

"Do you have ghost horses?" she asked.

Uncle Fig glanced at her. "Now there's something I haven't heard about in a while. Sure. At night, when there is just enough light from the moon, but not too much, only the white splotches of the Paint horses are noticeable. They appear to be floating. People who've seen them say they give them the shivers. Whether they're real ghosts or not depends on the believer." He winked at her.

Moose shook his head at his brother and slowed the vehicle to turn down a long dirt road. The truck crawled slowly, avoiding holes and ruts. A jackrabbit scampered across their path. The wind kicked up and sudden blasts whistled through the cab.

When Maya thought the road and the sagebrush would never end, she saw an old dilapidated trailer in a clearing between two hills. "Is that the camp?"

Uncle Fig laughed. "No. And we wouldn't put you in that rusty thing. That's an old campsite we used years ago, but it was a little too far from the river. We use the trailer for storage now."

They rounded a curve. Moose stopped the truck in the middle of the road. "Maya, look over there," he said, pointing out his window. "That's Aunt Vi's remuda. Ever heard that word? It means her group of horses. She chooses a mount from the group every day, alternating horses so one doesn't get too worn out or sore, especially if she's riding long distances."

Maya strained to look out. To the left, a large portable corral held five horses. In a connecting pen, one horse stood alone. In front of the corrals, a grass field stretched out with a worn dirt track.

Golly whined. Uncle Fig opened the passenger door so she could run ahead.

"Come on," said Moose. "Let's get out and say hello."

Maya hurried from the truck and ran to the corral,

gripping the sidebars. Mesmerized, she watched as the horses lumbered almost in slow motion, their regal heads much bigger than she had ever imagined, and their bodies massive and sobering. Tails swished at flies. Manes tossed and muscles twitched. Nostrils quivered as they snuffled and blew. Enormous eyes watched her, unconcerned. One horse rolled on the ground, legs in the air, rocking back and forth and causing a dust cloud. Another horse did the same, as if the first had given him the idea.

Maya smiled. They rolled in the dirt to keep flies off of them. From all of her visits to the library she had memorized a myriad of facts about horses. But all of the pictures in all of the books didn't compare to seeing them up close. Her eyes widened and she dared not blink for fear the vision before her would disappear.

Moose came up behind her and pointed at three

brown horses with black manes. "Those three are Russell, Catlin, and Homer. Their red-brown color is called 'bay.'"

"I know," said Maya.

"And Audubon is that light tan horse over there." Moose pointed to a horse taking a drink from a large trough. "Know what his color is called?"

"He's a dun." She pointed to the large gray. "And that's Seltzer, the blue roan. But he's not exactly blue. He's black and white all mixed together to look like he has a gray-blue tint. Did you know that the horse has the biggest eyeball of any land mammal?"

"Well, you sure know your horses," said Moose.

"I've only seen them in books. They're so much more . . . breathtaking in person." Maya pointed to the horse separated from the rest. "And that's a sorrel, right?"

Moose nodded. "A standard sorrel because everything's orange: coat, mane, and tail. That's Wilson, the horse Payton rides. I'm not sure why he's all by his lonesome. We'll have to ask Aunt Vi. Come on now. You'll have plenty of time to get to know the horses later. We'd better get to camp before she comes looking for us."

Reluctant to leave, Maya finally pulled away. In the truck, she knelt on the seat and looked out the back window. She could see her mother out here, hanging on the corral or sitting in the truck with Moose and Fig. She tried to imagine her father, too, but it was difficult to think of him anywhere but on Grandmother's arm and wearing a suit. Had he felt as she felt now? Amazed that there was a place so wide open?

When the horses disappeared from view, Maya turned around to see the camp spreading before her. A valley rested between a rocky mountain ridge and the coiling Sweetwater River, its banks caped in dense willows. Maya spied the tepees, like five little party hats scattered on a distant table of grass. As the truck edged closer, Maya saw two four-walled tents, side by side, their front flaps tied open. One was filled with cooking supplies: a larder of canned goods, wooden shelves crowded with pots, pans, and spires of dishes. An American flag dangled from the kitchen's tree-branch rigging. The other tent held a makeshift desk made from a sheet of plywood atop two sawhorses. A jumble of journals and reports fanned across the work area. Stacks of textbooks rose from the corners of the desktop. Rolled charts and maps huddled in corners.

Centered between both tents, a cast-iron pot hung from a tripod of poles over a fire pit surrounded by corrugated metal. Five white plastic chairs grinned around the nose of a small fire, as if cheerfully waiting for someone to sit down and visit.

Fig pointed to the office tent. "That's where Vi does her research and writes her articles. Most of those boxes in the back of the truck are headed for the office. She likes to have her books and papers with her wherever she goes. And speaking of your aunt Vi, here comes the Queen Bee now."

A woman charged through the willows and hurried toward them, cradling a bouquet of wildflowers in her arms. "I thought I heard the truck!"

Moose turned off the motor and they clamored from the cab.

Aunt Vi wore blue jeans, low-heeled boots, a crisp

white long-sleeved shirt, and a red silk kerchief tied in a low knot, like a necklace. The woman ignored Moose and Fig and grabbed Maya, holding her at arm's length.

"Finally, the girl cometh," said Aunt Vi. She pulled Maya in for a hug and rocked her back and forth.

Maya couldn't remember the last time someone had held her so long and squeezed her so tight, and even though she left her own arms dangling at her sides, she found herself leaning into Aunt Vi's embrace.

"I bet my pesky brothers have been filling your head with all sorts of twaddle about me. I'm glad to have another filly out here to balance out their nonsense." She released Maya and shoved the bouquet of wild-flowers into her hands.

It was hard to believe that Aunt Vi, Moose, and Fig

were brothers and sister because she was as short as they were tall. Her straw sun hat bore a gigantic brim that shaded her shoulders and was snug to her head with a stampede string. Every few moments the brim swelled with wind, threatening to lift her off the ground. The wind soon had its way and the hat flipped off her head backward, dangling and spinning from the safety of the leather braid. She had the same reddish hair as Uncle Fig, cropped almost as short, and the family's purplish eyes, but hers were accented in the corners with feathery white laugh lines.

Aunt Vi slapped her hands together and said, "Who feels alive in this wind? I sure do! Maya, you look so much like your mother, it's unsettling. Golly-girl, stop running in circles and sit!" The dog immediately complied. "Fig and Moose, if you don't mind, I need some wood hauled. I can split it later. Where's Payton? Payton! I sent him to the river and he's still not back." She hurried toward the truck, hoisted a box, and began carrying supplies into the tent.

Maya stood in the middle of the activity holding the flowers. She slowly turned in a circle and looked up at an endless and cavernous sky. There was far more heaven above her than there was earth below, and the horizon seemed worlds away. Without a white wall to define her boundaries, how would she ever know when she disappeared from someone's view?

Aunt Vi came out of a tent on her way to the truck for another load. "Maya, don't let that sky swallow you up. Put those flowers in a jelly jar in the kitchen tent.

The latrine is beyond those trees. That's our fancy word for a toilet in a tent. You probably need it after that long drive. Your tepee is over there." She pointed to a lone tent below the rock mountain. "Grab your suitcase from the truck and put it inside your tepee. After that, just sit in one of those chairs and relax until we get dinner ready. Tonight you're a guest. Tomorrow will be a different story." She hurried away.

Maya stared after Aunt Vi, intrigued by her exuberance, the way she bounded instead of walked, and the intense eyes that twinkled with excitement. She put the flowers in a jar with water and walked in the direction that Aunt Vi had pointed. She found a well-worn path in the grass that ended at a small clearing within a thicket of bushes.

The latrine was another tepee with an elevated wood box, fitted with a toilet seat and a roll of toilet paper on an upturned dowel. Maya tied the eight tent-flap ribbons to ensure privacy, then turned to face the makeshift bathroom. She pinched her nose closed and hesitated. Damp grass and dirt squished beneath her boots, and she hoped it was from groundwater. She squirmed, but there didn't seem to be an alternative.

As she untied the last of the tent ribbons to get out, something hissed and zoomed past her. "Who's there?" she called.

Maya heard sizzling, then a series of earsplitting bangs that sounded like gunfire. She covered her ears and screamed. Was someone shooting at her?

She flung herself forward, fell out of the opening, and landed facedown on the spongy ground.

12

A BOY DOUBLED OVER WITH LAUGHTER. "OH, THAT was so funny. . . ." He staggered around, giggling and pointing at her. "Look at you! You're covered in mud! Oh, that was great. That was just great." He dropped to the ground and rolled over. "I'm laughing so hard I'm crying." Slowly, he lifted himself, sighed, and wiped the tears from his dark blue eyes. "Hey. I'm Payton."

Maya spit damp grass from her mouth and swiped at her backside. So this was her cousin. She'd only been around Payton for one minute but could already tell he was an annoying nuisance, and she didn't like him. Maya narrowed her eyes and took a long, hard look at him. He was full-faced with deep dimples in both cheeks, shorter than Maya but not much, and sturdy. Bits of grass stuck in his blond hair, which was tousled from his hysterics. He wore jeans, boots, and a sweatshirt that read COWBOY UP! She turned and marched back toward the campsite.

He hurried behind her. "Hey! I *said*, 'I'm Payton!' Aren't you going to answer me? Where're your manners? Don't they have manners where you come from? Because it's not polite not to say hello."

Maya kept walking.

He ran to keep up, then turned, running backward alongside of her. "It was just some firecrackers. And they didn't make *that* much noise. No one can even hear them this far away from camp. Oh, I know. You're going to tell on me, aren't you? I knew you were a snitch the minute I saw you get out of the truck. That's all I need is a stupid girl out here who's a tattletale." His voice rose in pretend mockery. "'Aunt Vi, Aunt Vi, that mean boy threw

a firecracker at me.' That would be the disgusting worst."
He finally turned around, darted ahead, and then circled
back to keep pace with her. Maya had never seen anyone
so unsettled and who jigged around so much. Before she
reached the campsite, he finally stopped following her
and veered toward the corrals. Good, she thought. The
farther away, the better.

She walked to the truck, retrieved her suitcase and
her box of horses, and went to her tepee. Once inside,
she secured the flaps.

The tent smelled stale and was empty except for a
thick foam cushion on the canvas floor, a sleeping bag,
a pillow, and a stack of clothes. Maya unfolded two ker-
chiefs, a quilted vest, several pairs of shorts and jeans,
and a few T-shirts. The clothes weren't new, but as she
held them to her body, they seemed the right size.

She lifted the windbreaker-style jacket against her chest. It was much too big, but when she saw her mother's name written on the label, she didn't care. And even though she wasn't cold, she put it on, stroked the sleeves, and wondered if the other clothes had once belonged to her mother, too. Maya looked around the tiny cone-shaped room, took a deep breath, and thought of Grandmother. She would have been so appalled by the conditions. But Maya's mother had wanted this for her, and her father had agreed. There must be something wonderful here. She tied up the square window flap, retrieved several toy horses, and stood at the mesh screen looking out. Holding a horse figure to the portal, she whispered, "What's so special about this place?"

They ate around the fire: corn and chicken, fruit and potatoes. Moose and Fig washed the dishes in a big tub with water from the river that had been heated in a giant kettle while Aunt Vi wiped down the pantry. As the sun dipped behind the horizon, the sky smeared pink and orange and blue. Maya faced Payton, who sat across the fire, fiddling with a feather in his hand.

"I collect feathers. This is a magpie's. At home I have about fifty different ones. So if you see any, let me know and I'll tell you if I already have it or not."

Maya stared into the fire.

"By the way, ever ridden a horse?"

Maya glanced back. Fig and Moose and Aunt Vi were still occupied. "Sure," said Maya. "Lots of times."

"I've been riding since I was a kid," said Payton. "I've

got two horses at home and I've won all sorts of ribbons in juniors for barrel racing. Ever gone camping?"

She sighed and rolled her eyes. "Actually, I went to summer camp every year at Big Bear Lake. It was perfectly fun during the day with all the great activities, like swimming and crafts and hiking. We slept in tents until the bear came. . . ."

"A bear?" Payton leaned forward.

"Yes. A bear came into our camp in the middle of the night and ate all of our food and then totally destroyed the camp leader's tent. It's an absolute miracle he survived because the bear claws entirely ripped through the canvas. After that, they moved us to cabins."

"Wow. I guess that's why they call it Big Bear Lake, huh? I camp here every summer but we don't usually see bears. There are mountain lions around in the foothills looking for mule deer or pronghorn. When they find one, they follow it and then kill it, and try to hide it so they can come back and eat again later. By the way, ever felt any earthquakes? Because I hear they have them every couple of months where you live."

Maya forced a smile. "Actually, we have them every couple of *days*. We have to bolt down absolutely everything in the house or it just jiggles everywhere. And we have railings, so if you're walking down a street and there's an earthquake, you'll have something to grab on to. Once, I was upstairs and we had an earthquake and by the time it was over, it had tossed me all the way downstairs. It's extremely exciting and tremendously dangerous."

"Really? Do you . . . do you have to miss school?"

"Oh, sure. Because the classrooms are entirely in

shambles after an earthquake and we have to wait until they're cleaned up. Every year in June we have to make up all the days we missed for earthquakes. You know, earthquake days."

"Just like us making up snow days. Did you ever get hurt from one?"

Before she could answer, Aunt Vi, Fig, and Moose reassembled in their chairs with their coffee.

"What are you two talking about?" asked Vi.

"Maya was telling me about earthquakes," said Payton.

"You ever felt one?" asked Moose.

"Not really," said Maya.

Payton lurched forward in his chair. "But you just said —"

Maya interrupted him. "Grandmother told me that I slept through one once, but it didn't do any damage."

Aunt Vi glanced from Maya to Payton. "Okay then. Payton, how about running to my tent for my guitar?"

"Gladly," said Payton, giving Maya a mean smirk and nudging her chair as he walked by.

"Hurry back, Payton," called Moose. He turned to Aunt Vi. "Who would you like me to bell and hobble tonight?"

"Not Wilson," said Aunt Vi. "But Seltzer and Catlin could use a night out."

"What's bell and hobble?" asked Maya.

"I let a couple of horses out each night to graze around the campsite," said Aunt Vi. "I hobble them with a loose strap around their front legs so they can only take small steps. They can still get around pretty well but not too far. I put a cowbell on them, so we know where they are and because, to tell the truth, I like the sound. It's sort of reassuring to hear those clinks and clangs at night."

"What's the story on Wilson? Why's he separated from the rest?" asked Fig.

"He does this every summer when I first bring him out. I had him with the others for a few days, but when I try to take another horse through the gate, he is right there trying to edge through. Yesterday, he squeezed by and made it a mile before I caught him. I'll keep him separated until he gets used to his new surroundings and I can trust him not to take off. If he were hobbled, he'd just keep going all night and there's no telling where he'd be in the morning. Payton is going to have to keep that gate latched or Wilson might end up in California."

Payton returned, toting a black case and a songbook.

From the moment Aunt Vi opened the case and pulled out the burnished guitar, everything about her changed. As she tuned it, she became subdued and dreamy-eyed. She strummed and hummed, warming up her voice, then flipped through the book until she decided on a page. "Here's a song for Maya. It was Ellie's favorite." Her voice was round and smooth and she sang slowly, her words filled with melancholy.

Down in the valley, the valley so low

Hang your head over, hear the wind blow

Hear the wind blow, dear, hear the wind blow

Hang your head over, hear the wind blow.

Roses love sunshine, violets love dew

Angels in heaven know I love you

126

Know I love you, dear, know I love you

Angels in heaven, know I love you.

Maya heard a sniffle from Moose. She stole a quick glance at him and saw that he had pulled out his handkerchief. She knew how he felt. During Aunt Vi's song she had bitten her lip hard to keep her own longing for her mother at bay.

Aunt Vi turned a few pages in the book and started another song. She crooned about lost loves and people dying and lonesome trails. The tunes fit the mood, with the smoldering embers in the campfire and the encompassing quiet and the enormous darkening sky.

When she finished, even Payton seemed calmer. "Promise you'll sing every night, Aunt Vi?"

"I'll do my best, Payton." She looked at Maya. "I

tinker with the strings every evening. But when I'm heart-heavy, I only strum and can't bring myself to sing. There were a few years after your mother . . . when there was no singing." Aunt Vi busied herself with putting away the guitar.

Fig stood and stretched. Golly did the same. "It's about that time . . . Moose and I will be leaving early, Maya, so I'll see you in a few weeks. Have fun on Seltzer, your *Equus caballus*. Payton, I'm feeling a little scared-y. You'd better sleep in with me tonight."

Payton grinned and nodded.

"Good night, everyone. C'mon, Golly." Uncle Fig and his dog headed toward the river.

Moose stirred out the embers. "Vi, I'll take care of the horses." As he passed Maya's chair on his way to the corrals, he touched the top of her head and said,

"I never thought it would happen . . . you being on the Sweetwater with us. And I sure hate to leave you so soon. But we'll be back before you notice. Good night, Maya-bird. You don't mind if I call you that, do you?"

She shook her head, not minding at all.

"Well . . . okay then. I'm off to sleep." He disappeared in the darkness.

Aunt Vi pointed out where everyone slept. Moose, Fig, and Payton's tepees stood closest to the river; Aunt Vi's was in a clearing beyond the campfire; Maya's was farther away still. "If you need anything, just holler and I'll come running. In the morning, if I'm not in camp, get yourself some breakfast. The oatmeal will be on the warming grate over the fire. Then meet me up at the corrals. And Maya, Moose is right. We've missed you and we're very glad you're here."

Payton jumped up from his chair and, in his haste, knocked it over along with the one next to it. He quickly righted them and ran off, calling back, "Good night, Aunt Vi."

"Good night, Payton," she answered. Then more quietly, "That boy needs a big field and a bucking bronco to wear him out. Maya, I guess you can see that Payton's a bit of a tumbleweed. I'm not sure who looks forward to summertime more — Payton or his family." She handed Maya a flashlight. "Sleep tight, now."

"Thank you," said Maya, watching Aunt Vi walk away. She turned toward her tent and wished it wasn't so far from the others. She took tentative steps, following the beam of light. The darkness surrounded her. She tried to convince herself that there was a peacefulness about it, but Grandmother's stories about children disappearing in the night weaseled through. A shadow shifted. A willow branch snapped. She sensed a large presence nearby.

A low growl rumbled from the bushes.

She froze and gasped and swung the flashlight but could see nothing. Something thudded in front of her and then behind. She spun and finally shined the flashlight on the grinning Payton.

"Scare you?"

Maya gritted her teeth and marched around him toward her tepee.

He called after her in his fake voice, "Everyone's so happy you're here. . . . Maya this, Maya that . . . Just so you know, I'm *not* happy you're here."

Maya slipped into her tepee, tied all the flap ribbons, took off her boots, and crawled into her sleeping bag, fully dressed. She turned off her flashlight.

A creature wriggled across her legs! She jerked and tried to pull away. But it seemed to be everywhere at once. Maya jumped up and tripped from the confines of the mummy-like sleeping bag. As she struggled on the floor of the tent, tiny cold feet ran across her hand. She screamed, "Aunt Vi!"

When Aunt Vi finally untied the ribbons and forced her way inside the tent, she found Maya sitting motionless and shining her flashlight on a tiny mouse in the corner of the tepee.

"Maya . . . it's just a mouse. A little field mouse that couldn't hurt you." Aunt Vi shooed the mouse from the tent. "It looks like Payton's been up to his tricks again. Don't worry. It can't get back in."

"Are . . . are you sure?"

"Your tepee has a zipper beneath those ties," said Aunt Vi. "Fasten it tight and nothing can get inside."

Within moments, the strumming of tiny feet skittered up the outside of the tepee.

Aunt Vi reached up and slapped the side of the canvas.

Maya heard a simultaneous squeak and thud as the mouse hit the ground. She blew out a long breath.

"I'll have a talk with Payton, okay?" said Aunt Vi.

Maya nodded and zipped the tent opening after her. She inspected every crevice of the entire tent and inside the sleeping bag. Then she pulled deep into the quilted cocoon and wondered if it was possible to bell and hobble Payton.

13

MAYA FOLLOWED A PATH UP A DIRT HILL AND EMERGED in the field next to the remuda. She paused. The grass still glistened with morning dew, and the air was infused with the sweet grassy aroma of damp hay. As she approached the enclosures, several horses lifted their heads and whinnied.

She straightened the kerchief around her neck, snuggled her hands in the unzipped pockets of the vest, and whispered, "I'm going to ride a horse. A real horse." A spurt of excitement laced with anxiety coursed through her mind and her stomach. Would riding a horse feel the same as reading about riding a horse?

Curious about a blue plastic container a few feet from the corral, Maya stopped and lifted the lid.

Immediately, two horses edged as close to the bars as possible. Inside the container was some type of grain with a delicious smell that reminded Maya of oatmeal-and-molasses cookies. She scooped out a bit and with a cupped hand, fingers pointing up, held it through the bars. "Do you guys like this stuff?"

"Maya!"

She whirled around.

Aunt Vi hurried toward her.

"When you hold out your hand to a horse, especially if you have food in your hand, hold it flat and tight. A flat hand looks bigger. Believe me when I say that a horse could chomp those fingers and it wouldn't feel one bit good."

Maya swallowed hard. She turned back to the horse and leveled and tightened her hand. The horse deftly nibbled the food from her palm, its gigantic lips as tender as a baby's cheek.

"Okay. Let's get started. Follow me," said Aunt Vi.

"Where's Payton?" asked Maya as they entered the corral.

"After that prank last night, I told him to stay in camp during your lesson. You don't need more than one critic while you're learning. First thing, never sneak up on a horse or come up from the direct behind or the direct front, because they can't see you there. Most people approach a horse on the near side, which is their left. Always let them know you're coming."

Maya followed Aunt Vi into the corral, taking timid steps to avoid the occasional droppings.

"Hey there, Seltzer," said Aunt Vi. "I'm right here,

boy." She slipped the halter over the horse's muzzle and buckled it. "When you lead a horse, hold the rope a few inches from the halter clip, stand to the side, and walk as if you were the Queen of Sheba. You don't want to lead a horse by standing right in front of it because if it got spooked it would run right over you. Here, you take the rope and lead him to the tack bench."

Maya knew she wanted to try, so why was she hesitating? *Take the rope,* she told herself.

She wavered. Maybe it would be better to tell Aunt Vi that she'd rather wait until tomorrow or some other day.

Maya followed the rope from Aunt Vi's hand to the horse's face. She was surprised at the length of the lashes and the intense eye, which seemed to look through her and read her thoughts. There was something hypnotic about being in the horse's presence, as if she were under a spell. Was that her hand reaching for the rope? Was she the one leading Seltzer out of the corral to the tack bench? Or was it all a dream?

"There's an imaginary circle on the ground below the horse's shoulder," said Aunt Vi. "That's your safety zone for not getting run over or kicked. You can do most things to the horse from that spot on either side. Now we're going to groom the blanket area." She handed Maya a currycomb.

Maya copied Aunt Vi's small circular movements with a currycomb and then the long sweeping strokes with a dandy brush. She watched Aunt Vi use the hoof pick to pull out the packed dirt embedded in the horseshoes. Then they took turns combing the mane and tail.

"See how I put the blanket pads over the withers and his back and lift the saddle into place, letting it down lightly?" said Aunt Vi. "Now I'm going to drop the cinch and then come around . . . and thread the latigo strap through the rigging ring and tighten with short tugs. Now, the bridle. For your first few lessons, I'm going to put it on over the halter, so I can keep you on a lead rope."

Aunt Vi lifted the bridle over the horse's head, tickling the edges of the horse's mouth until it opened so the bit could slip inside. She fit the bridle over the ears. "Maya, you don't have to remember everything today, because you're going to hear me give you these directions thousands of times until it all becomes a habit and you can do it automatically. Understand?"

Maya nodded. She reached up and stroked the sleek

hair on Seltzer's neck and down toward his barrel. Standing so close, she felt an intense energy, yet at the same time an unusual calmness, as if she and the horse were somehow tied together and communicating in an ancient language. No wonder her mother had loved horses.

Aunt Vi helped her into the saddle and adjusted the stirrups. On a lead rope, Maya walked the horse in a large circle around Aunt Vi, first one direction and then the other. With each step, she felt the sway of Seltzer's shoulders.

"Now let's try a slow jog. Press on his sides with your legs and cluck to him."

"He won't go too fast, will he?" asked Maya. "Because I usually, almost always get migraine headaches if I go too fast."

"Maya, I have you on a lead rope. I'm not going to let the horse go too fast or get away from either one of us."

Maya clucked and Seltzer picked up speed. She felt the staccato of his jog. Aunt Vi had been right. It wasn't too fast at all. A wave of confidence washed over her, as if someone had given her a teaspoon of poise and self-assurance. For more than an hour she paid diligent attention to Aunt Vi's every instruction: Look out to where you want to go. Sit tall. Keep your heels down. Say *whoa* like you mean it.

After they removed Seltzer's tack and turned him into the corral, Maya wanted that feeling back. "When can I ride again?" she asked.

"Tomorrow morning and every day after," said Aunt Vi. "Now head back to camp. When you see Payton, send him up here. I'm going to work with him for a while. He's a different boy on a horse. Riding might as well be a tranquilizer for him, and I want him to find that quiet spot in his mind as much as possible. Don't forget your chores, Maya. Haul about a dozen pieces of wood from under the tarp to the pile next to the fire and then sweep out the kitchen tent, your tepee, and mine."

Maya nodded and ran back to the campsite, thinking that she was a different girl on a horse, too. Only for her, it wasn't a quiet spot. It was a happy, buoyant place. She called for Payton, but he didn't answer. She moved the wood for Aunt Vi and looked around the campsite again. Where was he? Maya took the broom to her tepee. When she lifted the flap, she saw that the lid was off her box of horses. The photo of her mother lay on the canvas floor. And the figures had disappeared. Maya ran toward Payton's tent.

She found him on a flat rock behind his tepee a few feet above the river, the horses in a pile next to him.

He held a miniature palomino in his hand. "Done with your pony ride? I bet you didn't even get off the lead rope."

"Those don't belong to you. Give . . . give them back." Her voice shook with anger. "Where's the brown-and-white Paint?"

He searched through the pile and held it up. "You mean this one?"

Maya walked closer. "Give it to me!"

Payton stood up, swung his arm back, and threw the brown-and-white horse into the dense willows.

"No!" Maya ran to the spot where she thought it had landed. She pushed her way into the bushes and searched the ground near the bank. She swept the dried leaves away, saw what she thought was the horse, but instead brought up a handful of twigs. She continued in a frantic scramble, whimpering, "I can't lose her. . . . She's all I have left. . . ." Willow limbs smacked her face. She pulled out from underneath the bushes, stood up, and looked at the deep and endless hedges. It would take forever to find it. Tears streamed down her dusty cheeks, leaving muddy tracks.

Payton came up behind her. "What's the big deal, anyway?"

She wiped away her tears and turned to face him, her fists clenching and unclenching. "It was . . . It was mine. . . ."

Payton taunted her. "If you're so sad and you don't like this place, make sure you tell Aunt Vi. Because I heard her talking to Moose this morning and he said that when he comes back, if this is all too much for you, he'll take you to the ranch. Isn't that great? You can leave. All you have to do is tell Aunt Vi that you hate it here. Then maybe things can get back to the way they should be, with just me and my grandpa Fig, and my uncle Moose and my aunt Vi." He turned and ran.

Maya hurried to the flat rock and collected the remaining horses in her kerchief and walked toward camp, swaddling the bundle next to her body. A wave of tears started again. She muttered under her breath. "I don't hate it here. I hate . . . *you*."

"You're sure quiet this evening, Maya," said Aunt Vi. "You didn't come out of your tent all afternoon and barely touched your dinner."

Payton leaned forward in his chair, his voice dripping with fake concern. "Yeah, Maya, are you okay?"

Maya pulled farther into her jacket. Payton would just love it if she spilled her guts to Aunt Vi, but she wasn't about to give him that satisfaction. "Just tired, I guess."

"You have every right to be tired," said Aunt Vi. "You've had more changes in the last week than most people have in ten years. On top of all that, today was your first day on a horse. Let's get to bed early. Payton, did you check the horses?"

"Yes. I belled and hobbled Catlin and Audubon."

"You latched Wilson's gate?"

"Yes, ma'am."

Maya gazed toward the corrals.

"Maya, stir out that fire. Payton, help me wipe down the kitchen. Then let's turn in."

After Aunt Vi and Payton left, Maya stood for a long time jabbing at the embers, which occasionally pulsed with a hot red glow. The wheels of resentment churned in her mind for everything Payton had: his parents, his brothers, an entire life of riding horses. He'd even had Aunt Vi, Fig, and Moose every summer. Maya gritted her teeth, pressed her lips together, and shook her head.

When the embers quieted, she laid down the poker and headed toward the latrine tent, shining the flashlight down the path. But by the time she arrived, an idea had blossomed. She diverted behind the latrine tent and turned off the beam.

Maybe if Aunt Vi saw how careless Payton was, she would send *him* back to the ranch for the rest of the summer. Maya smiled at that delicious possibility.

Lope

14

Maya's sleep went undisturbed. After the flurry, travel, and exhaustion of the last few days, nothing stirred her. Not the high-pitched songs of the coyotes, the clangs of the hobbled horses, or the *thwap* of the tepee billowing with the wind. It wasn't until she heard the revving of a motor that she awoke.

As she dressed, Maya felt an unfamiliar tightening and soreness of the muscles on the insides of her legs, but she decided not to mention it to Aunt Vi. She didn't want anything to interfere with her lessons.

Maya walked slowly and stiffly to the breakfast campfire, where she found Aunt Vi staring into her coffee. On the hill, an unfamiliar truck hitched to a horse trailer pulled away from the corral area. "Who's that?" she asked.

Aunt Vi let out a long breath. "The vet. Wilson escaped last night. He wandered and must have caught a leg in a badger hole. Somehow, he limped back here but then went down. I drove to a neighbor's ranch early this morning and called the vet. She's taking him to her ranch until his leg heals." Aunt Vi looked at Maya, mystified. "Payton loves that horse and takes better care of him every summer than I do all year long."

Maya chewed on the inside of her lip.

A few minutes later, Payton walked into camp, his head down, and his face blotchy and red. He sank into one of the chairs. "Aunt Vi, I am so sorry. I swear I latched that gate last night. I swear."

"No need for swearing. You were in a hurry and didn't pay attention."

"No! I checked it twice. I promise." His eyes pleaded for belief.

Maya sat on the edge of a chair and stared at the ground, stirring the dirt with the toe of one boot. She looked up and caught Aunt Vi studying her with a questioning gaze. Maya quickly averted her eyes and stood up, holding her hands out to warm them over the fire.

Aunt Vi directed her words to Payton but she continued to stare at Maya. "I'm surprised at you, Payton. Being so careless . . . It just broke my heart to see poor Wilson suffering with so much pain, his big eyes looking at me for relief, and all his moaning and confusion. You know, a horse's greatest fear is different from a human's. Our innate fear is of falling. But a horse's is of not being able to get up and flee from danger or a preda-tor. Imagine what that poor animal felt. . . ."

Payton dropped his head into his hands and sobbed.

Maya's face wrenched with remorse. "Aunt Vi . . . I . . . I might have . . ."

Payton raised his head and looked at her. "Wait a minute. . . . You! You did it to get back at me! Because of the stupid plastic horses!"

Maya's anger swelled. "They're not stupid plastic horses! My *mother* gave them to me!"

Aunt Vi nodded. She blew out a long breath. "Maya, there's never been a Limner who would endanger the life of a horse."

Maya's stomach felt sick with desperation. Her words scrambled. "I . . . I didn't mean for it to happen.

I actually just went up to say good night to the horses and . . . and . . . Wilson came over toward me completely on his own. He . . . acted extremely hungry so I gave him some of the molasses grain, just like you showed me, Aunt Vi. And I guess . . . when I leaned over the gate, the latch must have caught on my jacket . . . or something entirely innocent like that."

"You're a liar!" Payton jumped up and held up a fist.

"That's enough," said Aunt Vi. "Maya, what did Payton do to you that would warrant this?"

Maya's thoughts bunched so tight that she couldn't pry them apart. Aunt Vi didn't understand. Nobody understood. Maya spit out the words. "Nothing," she said. "He did positively . . . absolutely nothing."

"Is that true, Payton? You've done nothing to make Maya angry?"

Payton shifted in his chair and hung his head.

Aunt Vi studied both of them and shook her head with disgust. "So both of you have treated the other with disrespect."

"Aunt Vi," Maya said with earnestness, "you can banish me to my tepee if you want. I'm perfectly comfortable being by myself. I'm not used to being around boys of any kind. I don't understand about teasing or being obnoxious or any of the unsavory and mean things they do, so it's fine with me if you need to separate us and send Payton away. I am truly sorry for my inconsiderate behavior, but it was absolutely . . . an accident. I hope you'll forgive me."

Aunt Vi tossed the remains of her coffee in the fire and paced. She finally stopped and glared at Maya. "I'd like to believe you, but I don't. And for the time being, neither one of you is forgiven, or going anywhere. Starting now, you'll do just about everything together. You will eat facing each other. You will do any number of chores I can dream up, together. Payton, you will be Maya's groom at her lesson, and Maya, you will be Payton's groom at his. And if either of you fails to cooperate or if one impolite word passes between you, you'll do nothing else but shovel manure . . . together."

Maya nodded. "Don't worry, Aunt Vi. I'm actually not going to speak to him ever again."

"Me neither," added Payton.

"Suit yourselves," said Aunt Vi. "But you're going to get tired of hearing my voice."

Maya and Payton peeled carrots and potatoes, washed dishes, raked the clearing, soaped bridles and saddles, swept out the tents, and toted buckets of water from the river to the campsite, side by side. By the afternoon of the sixth day, not an utterance had passed between them and their mutual stubbornness seemed indestructible.

As Maya helped Payton stack wood near the campfire, she caught Aunt Vi watching them. Maya raised her chin in the air and walked back toward the woodpile. Payton walked next to her, staring at the ground. Later, in the corral before Maya's lesson, Payton handed Seltzer's reins to Maya without even looking at her. Maya snatched the leather straps from him and turned away to find Aunt Vi studying them again.

Aunt Vi's eyes narrowed. Her mouth set in a straight line and her head nodded almost imperceptibly, as if she'd made up her mind about something. "Let's get started!" she called, rubbing her hands together.

Aunt Vi barked out orders. Maya walked Seltzer, jogged him, backed up, side passed, and wove in serpentine patterns around poles. Then, on Aunt Vi's command, she repeated the sequences. After the long lesson, Aunt Vi turned and headed toward the corral gate. Maya dismounted and wiped the sweat trickling down her neck with her kerchief.

Aunt Vi jerked around. "We're not stopping, Maya. I know you've been on the horse for almost two hours but you're not done yet. Get back up there. You're going to lope."

"But I'm tired and I've never loped before. . . ."

"Most members of this family learn before they go to kindergarten. Don't you think you've got some catching up to do? Now get back on that horse. Do you want to be the first Limner who doesn't know how to lope?"

Why was Aunt Vi being so mean? Maya climbed back into the saddle. "I just . . . don't want to go too fast."

"Why do you panic every time I ask you pick up a little speed? What is it now, Maya?"

What was the matter with Aunt Vi? Why was she grilling her? For the entire lesson, nothing had seemed good enough, and she hadn't given even the tiniest approval. "Going fast makes me feel sick. I actually . . . get motion sickness. . . ."

Aunt Vi put her hands on her hips. "Bring him to a jog. Collect his head. Press your leg on his right side, a little farther back than normal. And make the sound of a kiss."

With reluctance, Maya attempted Aunt Vi's directives. Seltzer made a sudden rise in the air and back down. Like a merry-go-round horse, he jolted up and down, up and down, then faster and faster.

Aunt Vi yelled, "Let go of the horn! Stay centered. Heels down. Keep your back flexible. Your arms are flapping all over the place! Look where you're headed, not down at the ground. Don't let your bottom slap. Oh, for heaven's sake, say 'whoa!'"

"Whoa!" Maya and Seltzer came to an abrupt stop, and she almost tumbled over the horn.

"That was messy," said Aunt Vi. "You can do better. Try again."

Shaken, Maya whined, "I want to get off."

"Again!" said Aunt Vi.

Maya frowned but she brought the horse to a jog and gave the cue. She kept her leg on his side, forgetting to remove it, and Seltzer loped in tight circles.

"Maya! What are you doing? Give the cue and release. Now start over!"

"He's not doing it right!" Maya complained.

Aunt Vi's eyes pierced through her. "*You're* not doing it right!"

Maya clucked to bring Seltzer to a jog and they headed down the straightaway. A cottontail jumped from a nearby sagebrush and darted in front of them, its white tail bobbing.

Seltzer reared.

Maya felt her body lift high into the air and slide from the saddle. Her boots slipped from the stirrups. She dropped the reins. A frightening, sinking feeling came over her. She plummeted and her body smacked the dirt. Would the horse fall on her? Was she going to die?

She heard Seltzer's hooves retreating.

Payton jumped from the fence and reached Maya first. "Are you okay?"

Maya stared at his boots and felt him taking her arm. She rolled over, shaking, and sat up.

"Get up," said Aunt Vi as she approached. "Payton, run and get her horse. Maya, you and Seltzer have some unlearning to do before we stop for the day."

"Aunt Vi, she might be hurt," said Payton.

"Get the horse, Payton."

Maya felt tears oozing from her eyes. "I can't. Seltzer threw me. . . ."

"He didn't throw you. You fell. Think like a horse. Horses are prey animals. Their main goals in life are to graze, stay with the herd, and flee from danger. Seltzer thought the rabbit was a predator. *You* know it was a little rabbit, but *he* thought it was a mountain lion. Sooner or later, most horses do something unpredictable. If you had been looking out instead of down, and if you had been balanced and centered in your seat, you wouldn't have fallen when he reared."

Payton brought Seltzer around and held out the reins. Aunt Vi stood nearby with her arms crossed.

Sweat rivulets streamed down Maya's back, and dust stuck to her arms and cheek. Her voice filled with anger and frustration at Aunt Vi. "Don't you understand? I told you. I have . . . motion sickness. I get extremely sick on roller coasters and motorcycles and trains . . . and . . ."

"When did you ride any of those things?" interrupted Aunt Vi. "Your grandmother's lawyer told Moose that you were barely allowed out of the house for six years. That you were practically a prisoner . . ."

Furious tears spewed. "You don't know what I've done!" said Maya. "I've had lots of opportunities! Grandmother took me to amusement parks all the time, usually once a month. And she let me ride on the back of a neighbor's motorbike, entirely for fun. And I rode a train when we went on vacation . . . to . . . to San Juan Capistrano! But I only did those things once because they made me throw up. And . . . and anything fast brings back all the horribly awful memories about the tragedy that happened to my parents, because the driver of the other car was unnecessarily speeding!"

Aunt Vi shook her head. "Listen to yourself. You're just making things up as you go along. There was no other car. Your parents' car skidded during a rainstorm and ran into a mountain. Are you going to use their deaths as an excuse for everything that you can't do or are afraid to try, for the rest of your life? Because Maya, if so, you'll be painting yourself into a corner with all of your lies and you'll be stuck without ability or experience. Your parents died. You never have to get over it, but you do have to get *on* with it." Aunt Vi yelled so loud that a sage grouse flew out of a nearby bush. "Now get up and get back on that horse!"

Payton's forehead furrowed with concern. "Aunt Vi, you're being kind of mean. . . ."

Aunt Vi turned on Payton. "Payton, who are you to be talking to me about being mean to Maya? There's not *one* of us leaving here until she lopes. So if you've got any comments, give them to Maya in the form of a suggestion."

Frowning, Payton backed away.

"Get on that horse, Maya," said Aunt Vi.

Maya saw a flicker of loathing in Aunt Vi's eyes and it pried the lid on her resolve. Remarks flashed in her mind. *Most members of this family learn to lope before they go to kindergarten. The Limners were born to ride. There's not one of us who didn't take to the saddle.* Maya stood and took the reins.

Payton rushed forward and held the stirrup for her. He whispered, "I know Aunt Vi. We'll be here until you get it right, even till midnight."

Maya put her foot in the stirrup, grabbed the horn, and hoisted herself into the seat.

Payton looked up at her. "If Seltzer goes too fast, just pull back on the reins so the bit makes contact with his mouth, then release. Just bump and release."

Maya nodded to him. She brought the horse to a jog, gave the leg cue, and made the sound of a kiss. The transition felt gentler his time. She stayed on.

"Now ride!" yelled Aunt Vi. "Ride like someone is trying to catch you. Ride!"

Maya looked ahead through Seltzer's ears and held the reins in front of the horn. She kept her arms still and close to her body, her legs positioned with heels down, and stayed centered. The horse's hooves pounded out a tempo like the sequential thrumming of fingers. Maya flew down the dirt track and through the turn, the breeze amusing her cheeks. She rode, giving Seltzer more leg, and he picked up speed. The perfect metrical beat of the horse's stride became the rhythm of her own breathing. *Hoosh, hoosh, hoosh.* In those moments, nothing that had happened before, or might happen after, mattered. She was flooded with an unfamiliar yet lucid happiness. She wanted to lope and lope and lope forever.

When Maya dismounted, she was breathless and her face felt flushed.

Aunt Vi dashed forward and Maya smiled, expecting

167

congratulations. Instead, Aunt Vi took Seltzer's reins.

"Payton! Maya! Change into shorts and an undershirt and meet me at the river." She turned away, leading the horse toward the corral.

Maya stared after her. "Didn't I do it right?"

"Yeah. You did fine," said Payton. "She's probably going to make us scrub river rocks. She made me do that once when I talked back to her."

15

Aunt Vi strode toward them with towels in one hand and a bottle of shampoo in the other. She wore her cowboy boots and a bathing suit with a long work shirt as a cover-up, which was as long as a dress on her short body. "This way!" she said, and took off toward the willows, walking as if she were about to miss a bus.

Maya and Payton trudged after her, trying to keep up. They followed along the bank of the river until they reached a grassy overlook, elevated a few feet above a pool in the river.

Aunt Vi stopped and tossed towels at Maya and Payton. "You're both getting a little ripe." She nodded toward the river. "Payton, don't you think it's time Maya had a camp baptism? Maya, there's nothing better than the soft water of the Sweetwater."

"Yes!" said Payton. He dropped to the ground, pulled off his boots and socks, and jumped from the bank. A giant splash followed.

Maya stared at Aunt Vi, puzzled. They weren't going to wash river rocks?

"Can you swim?" asked Aunt Vi, taking off her shirt and starting on her boots.

Maya looked down at her filthy arm. She had wondered if she was ever going to take a bath again. Since she'd arrived there'd been nothing more than a daily washing over a bowl of water and a swipe here and there with a washcloth. "Yes, I can swim," she said, then added with a nervous laugh, "but . . . I don't know about this. . . ." Maya dropped to the grass anyway, tugging on her boots and releasing her hair from the ponytail.

Aunt Vi scuttled down the embankment and into the water.

"Come on!" yelled Payton. "It's easier than falling off a horse." He dove under.

Maya took timid steps on the bank. "I can't believe I'm doing this. I really can't believe I'm doing this." She stood shivering on the bank, held her nose with one hand, closed her eyes, and jumped. She plunged into the clear water and then sprang back up, screaming at its coldness.

Payton laughed.

Maya laughed, too, as surprised by the sound of her own giggling voice as she was by the icy river.

Aunt Vi grinned and tossed her the shampoo.

Maya treaded water and then swam to a shallow spot on a sandbar. She sat down and squirted the shampoo on her head. When it was foamy, she squished it from her hair and massaged it all over her body, then dipped under, again and again, until the soap disappeared. I'm taking a bath in a river, she thought, and couldn't help but wonder what Grandmother would think. But Maya didn't care. She had never been so dirty or felt so clean.

Maya followed Aunt Vi out of the river. They spread their towels on the bank, side by side, and sat on them. The warm breeze dried their bodies.

Payton scaled up the bank and jumped back into the river, displacing a fair amount of water. When he sprang up, he waved.

Aunt Vi waved back and continued to watch him. "You know, Maya, when Payton's at home, his three brothers tease him to distraction. On top of that, they're all star athletes. They're good riders, too, but Payton outshines them in competitions. I try to coach him as much as I can so he has one thing he's better at than they are. He's usually a more settled soul out here than he is at home." Aunt Vi leaned over and nudged Maya with her elbow. "But I think you threw a monkey wrench in his summer. Don't worry, he'll adjust. Wide-open space does that to people. Slows them down and gives them time and legroom to sort out their thoughts and put them in the right order."

Maya watched Payton swim toward a deeper pool farther upstream. She tried to imagine what it would be like to have three older brothers who tormented her.

"He's a good swimmer," said Maya.

"He's good at a lot of things. At home, he just gets a little lost in the shuffle. Where did you learn to swim?" asked Aunt Vi.

"I had swimming lessons at one of my schools."

Aunt Vi turned her head to look at Maya. "Is that the truth?"

Maya nodded, her eyes large and sincere. "One of my schools offered lessons and Grandmother allowed it because swimming is related to safety. She always worried that I might drown in the bathtub or a puddle or that there might be a flood. She . . . she worried about so many dreadful things."

"She must have loved you very much," said Aunt Vi.

Maya gave her a curious look.

"She wouldn't have gone to so much trouble to pro-tect you if she hadn't cared about you," said Aunt Vi.

It had never occurred to Maya that Grandmother's behavior was a form of love. "But she acted so mean . . . and she hated my mother. I wasn't even allowed to say her name or I'd get in trouble. Grandmother got rid of all of my mother's pictures, except for one that I kept hidden, and she said . . . she said that my mother took her son away from her . . . and killed him."

A tiny frown crowded Aunt Vi's forehead. "I had no idea, Maya. All I can say is that she must have needed somebody to blame for your father's death. Probably made it easier for her. In a way, sadness is proof of how much you cared for the person who died, so it's hard to move away from it. Some people get stuck in their sorrow and grab on much too tight to what they have left. The lawyer told Moose that your grandmother closed herself off from the entire world and tried to do the same to you. That makes me think she was just sad and afraid. I have to feel sorry for someone like that."

"Was Moose ever sad and afraid when my mother died?"

"Sure. We all were. But we had each other to lean on and to share the sadness. We dragged each other out of the wallow so it was easier to get on with laughing and loving . . . and singing."

"He still seems sad," said Maya.

"Oh, that's because Moose wears his heart on his sleeve. Know what that means?"

Maya shook her head.

"It means he wears his feelings on the outside instead

of covered up on the inside. He gets emotional when he's sad *and* when he's happy. And during a beautiful sunset. Or at the drop of a hat." Aunt Vi smiled.

"His wife died, too, right? My other grandmother?" said Maya.

"Yes, we lost Moose's wife many years ago when your mother was just a baby."

"So . . . my mother didn't have a mother, either . . . just like me."

"Yes and no. Back then, I was a young woman just out of grad school, teaching art history at a university in the East. When Moose's wife died, I came home to help raise Ellie. She was my niece, and she needed me. I never regretted it. Secretly, I had missed my family and my horses but was too proud to admit it to anyone. Fig joined us when he became a widower, but even when he didn't live at the ranch, he and his family were around all the time. We all played a part in raising Ellie. I guess I filled in as her mother."

Aunt Vi sat up, leaned her elbows on her knees, and stared downstream, where Payton stood on the bank, skipping rocks into the river.

Maya followed her gaze, thinking about how much Aunt Vi, Uncle Fig, and Moose must have loved her mother, too.

"Your mother used to say that the Sweetwater wore a hole in her heart that she could never fill up with contentment from anywhere else. This spot was one of her favorite places, Maya. Here, and being out with the wild horses. You'll see why tomorrow."

"Tomorrow?"

"I'm taking you and Payton to see a harem band I've

been watching. I keep track of several of the smaller harems so that when I take groups out, I'll know where they are. We'll probably see one or two of the stallions your father painted. He was a talented artist. You must have known that."

Maya shook her head. "Grandmother said she destroyed everything. The only painting of his I've ever seen is the one in the living room at the ranch."

Aunt Vi's mouth set in a straight line and she shook her head. "All his beautiful paintings . . . well . . . I can at least show you what inspired him, and if we're lucky, you'll see the brown-and-white Paint your mother once rode."

"That's . . . that's the picture I have. . . . She's on a brown-and-white horse!"

"The horse's name is Artemisia," said Aunt Vi. "She

was a yearling who was separated from her mother during a gather and taken to auction."

"What's a gather?"

"It's a polite word for a roundup. I bought Artemisia and trained her for three years. She was a four-year-old, just like you, that last summer you and your mom visited. Ellie adored that horse and rode her the entire time she was here. She was my horse, Maya, but Artemisia and your mother had a connection like I've never seen before. When Ellie left, Artemisia pined for days. Later that summer, I moved Artemisia out here to the Sweetwater because I needed more remuda horses to outfit and guide a pack trip for a group of photographers. I let someone else ride Artemisia. That was my mistake."

"Why?"

"We had been out all day, tracking a band of wild horses," said Aunt Vi. "When we set up camp for the night, I was busy putting up a portable corral, and the photographers were taking off their horses' tack. The woman riding Artemisia forgot to half-hitch a halter around Artemisia's neck before she removed the bridle. About that time, a stallion with his harem came over a ridge almost in our laps. All those photographers went crazy, grabbing their cameras and shooting pictures. After it was all said and done, the woman noticed Artemisia had wandered off. By then, the stallion was already circling and posturing. He came up from behind and snaked Artemisia away, right out from under our noses. I was heartsick until I was able to see how well she adapted back to the wild. I spotted her a few weeks ago, right after she foaled. She has a new colt. I named him Klee."

"Klee," repeated Maya. "That's a funny name."

"I name the horses after famous painters."

"How come?"

Aunt Vi leaned back on her elbows, and her eyes turned wistful, like when she sang around the campfire. "Look around. Out here in all this bigness, every single thing matters and stands out. When the horses run against the wind with their manes and tails flying, I think they look like fleeting brushstrokes of color. I consider them the artists on this enormous outdoor canvas, making it more beautiful. So I name them so. The male horses get last names and the females get first names just so we can keep the genders straight. I'm partial to painters of the American Southwest. Others are favorites whose lives I admire or artists I teach in my classes."

Payton emerged from the bushes on the edge of the clearing. "Look what I found!" He ran toward them, a skinny black snake dangling from his hands.

"Payton . . . ?" warned Aunt Vi.

He veered away and released the snake beneath an outlying willow bush. Aunt Vi shook her head and smiled at Maya. "A few days ago that might have ended up in your tent. There might be hope for that boy yet."

As Maya dressed, she said, "Aunt Vi, I . . . I did unlatch the gate . . . on purpose."

Aunt Vi nodded and pulled on her boots. "I know. Thank you for owning up. And Maya, I was a little hard on you today . . . on purpose. I didn't expect you to fall, though. You gave me a scare. But you did good anyway. You're a natural, just like a Limner."

As Maya followed Aunt Vi back to camp, she hugged her towel. She couldn't stop thinking about everything Aunt Vi had said. About her mother and the river and the wild horses. And about being a Limner. Her face pinked from the afternoon sun, but she beamed as much on the inside as she did on the out.

16

ARTEMISIA LED THE FAMILY TOWARD THE GULCH. KLEE high-stepped next to her with sprightly freedom. Since his birth only a few weeks ago, he had grown and filled out, his hair now fluffy with thick whorls of brown and white. With newfound bravado, Klee tried to prance in front of Artemisia, but she crowded his progress until he stopped. Georgia jogged forward to babysit, keeping Klee a safe distance behind their pilot.

As the band moved into the lowlands closer to the water hole, three figures appeared on the rise of the hill. Artemisia stopped and raised her head in their direction, ears alert. One was the familiar woman, who often watched them for hours but had never been a threat. Sargent's ears twitched upright and he whinnied as if asking, "Is everything all right?" Artemisia whinnied back to him with reassurance and continued toward the drinking spot. Sargent wasn't satisfied and continued to stare at the observers. His authoritative posture announced, "Don't approach or you will have to deal with me." When he sensed no danger, he followed the band.

Artemisia noticed that Mary, who was known to dally, slowed behind the rest, but then saw Sargent come up from behind and bite her on the flank. Mary loped forward to keep up with the others. Everyone was accounted for, except Wyeth.

Artemisia heard Wyeth's whinny and looked toward the foothills. He stood alone, calling to them. He jogged forward, but Sargent turned suddenly, arched his neck, snorted, and pawed at the ground. Wyeth retreated to a small knoll, turning his head one way and then the other.

Wyeth was more than two years old now. It was time for him

to be on his own; to find a band of bachelor stallions with whom he'd live in fraternity; to pretend fight, play rough, and chase the others with his neck outstretched in the snaking posture. It would all be a rehearsal for when he was older and strong enough to challenge a stallion with a harem, win a mare, and start his own family. Artemisia watched as Wyeth again took tentative steps in their direction. Sargent lunged toward him with an angry squeal. Even though Wyeth was Georgia's son and had been in the band since birth, Artemisia and the other mares knew better than to interfere with Sargent's fierce rejection and seemed resigned to Wyeth's exile. Finally, he hung his head and disappeared over the hill. For the first time in his life, he had to choose his own path.

Artemisia turned her attention to the others. Georgia and Mary dropped to the water and rolled. Artemisia did the *same and Klee copied her. She stood and walked from the water.*

Klee followed. Both shook off a rain of droplets. Artemisia

nuzzled his face as if trying to absorb his presence. She draped

her neck over his withers, reassuring herself that he wasn't

going anywhere with a band of bachelor stallions, at least

for now.

17

"Stay close to me and away from that drop-off," said Aunt Vi. "I am not ready to lose either of you to the Great Divide Basin."

Maya, Aunt Vi, and Payton sat on their horses at an overlook and gazed out at the infinite crater of desert. Below them, the Honeycomb Buttes rose abruptly from the basin floor in peculiar sandstone spires of rust, brown, and green. In the east, Continental Peak saluted, and in the west, the Oregon Buttes lay like a sleeping giant.

"Have you ever seen anything like it?" asked Aunt Vi.

Maya shook her head. She might as well have been on an alien planet. Was she really here? On her way to see the wild horses? She'd hardly been able to sleep last night for thinking about this very moment. First thing this morning, Aunt Vi had been surprised to find her warming her hands over the campfire, already dressed and waiting. After breakfast, they had loaded Russell, Homer, and Seltzer into the gooseneck trailer, and Aunt Vi had driven Maya and Payton south along the Continental Divide.

Now, Aunt Vi turned her horse north, and Maya and Payton followed on theirs. The mirage of a shimmering lake appeared before them, but as they rode closer, it vanished. What Maya thought was a congregation of rocks on a hillside manifested into a herd of pronghorn. She gasped and chills ran up her arms as she watched them flee across the panorama in a graceful, white-bottomed ballet.

"It's a mysterious place out here, Maya. I'm always amazed, too, at the beauty and the strangeness of it all."

Maya nodded and felt an odd expectation, as if something unusual might happen at any moment. She knew it was a ridiculous notion, but she imagined that when she caught her first glimpse of Artemisia, she might see her mother sitting on the horse, too. Or would at least feel her presence. Out here, where the eye played tricks, it almost seemed possible.

They stopped, dismounted, haltered the horses, and tied them to the woody sagebrush. Aunt Vi led them to the crest of a hill above Oregon Gulch where they sat cross-legged, waiting.

"Aunt Vi, are there any ghost horses out here?" asked Maya.

Aunt Vi smiled. "Who told you about ghost horses?"

"My mother . . . She said the only way to capture a ghost horse is to paint the tail of the wind."

"I can paint the wind," said Payton. "Want me to show her how fast I can ride, Aunt Vi?"

"Payton, we just sat down. Now stay put. All you'd do is scare off every living thing for miles. There are a lot of ghosts out here, including Artemisia. It's that stark white coat against the darkness that makes believers out of skeptics." Aunt Vi almost whispered, "She's the most beautiful, though."

"Aunt Vi, why can't you just take Artemisia back if she belonged to you?" asked Maya.

"Payton, why?"

"Because it would be too dangerous," said Payton.

"That's right. I'd need a group of wranglers to separate her from a possessive stallion. She was born wild and knows how to survive out here, so I've let her be. That decision wasn't easy, though. And I miss her."

"Won't the wild horses try to steal our horses?"

"No way," said Payton. "They only try to steal mares. Our horses are boy horses, and the stallion has to be the only grown-up boy in a wild horse family. He doesn't like any competition. If another male horse came close, he would fight him and drive him away. Sometimes, one stallion tries to steal another stallion's mare and then there's a giant fight and they rear and bite each other and kick each other and there's blood. . . ."

Aunt Vi put a hand on Payton's arm to settle him. She lifted her glasses. "Look. There's a family in the distance heading toward the water hole. Stay nice and still. No sudden moves."

Maya's mouth wetted with anticipation and she licked her lips. She looked through the binoculars and saw five horses emerge between the hollow of two hills.

Aunt Vi whispered, "There's Sargent, the stallion. He's the palomino behind the rest of them. Isn't he beautiful?"

Sargent reminded Maya of the landscape, raw and untamed. His coat was marked with nicks and scars, his forelock dangling in stringy moplike bangs.

"And see the flaxen mare? That's Georgia. And there's Mary, the two-year-old. She looks more like Sargent with that palomino color. Artemisia is right in the front. Do you see her, Maya?"

Maya held her breath and then reminded herself to exhale. She leaned forward and tried to hone in on Artemisia, but the horse appeared blurry through the lenses. Maya took a deep breath to calm herself as she focused the binoculars. The image sharpened.

Artemisia didn't have the sleek look of the remuda

horses or the groomed and trimmed face of the horse she had seen in the photo. Witches' knots tangled her mane and tail, dirt crusted on her round barrel, and her legs and face were shaggy with wispy hairs. But even so, there was a strength of character about her, in the way she walked, in the way she held her head with royal forbearance.

Artemisia gazed toward Maya as if she were looking directly through the binoculars and into her eyes.

Something fluttered deep inside Maya. "She knows we're here."

"She knows and so do Sargent and the others. But they're used to me watching them and bringing people around. I like to think that Artemisia remembers me. Maybe something about my body posture or my scent." Aunt Vi's voice caught with affection. "Oh, Maya, look right behind Artemisia, between the other two mares. There's the foal, Klee."

Klee stood out in contrast to the others: His hair looked new and soft and fluffy, his face animated and almost whimsical. Maya wished she were close enough to touch him. She couldn't take her eyes from his antics and found herself smiling. He was so curious and filled with spunk, and he seemed to love his mother with brazen adoration.

Aunt Vi scanned with the binoculars. "Where's Wyeth?"

"I see him," said Payton. "See, Aunt Vi? Over on that hill. He's trying to come to the water hole, but Sargent won't let him."

"It's time," said Aunt Vi.

Maya shifted her gaze and saw the lone horse wander away. "Time for what?" she asked.

"To leave the family. The stallion drives the mature males away when they're between two and three years old, to prevent inbreeding. And because the young male's desire is to be rambunctious and disruptive. Ever heard the phrase 'sow his wild oats'? That's what Wyeth will do now, until he's ready to settle down."

"Aunt Vi," said Payton. "Can I ride back?"

"Go ahead. Keep Homer steady at the lope and don't let him work into a gallop."

"Yes! Meet you at the trailer." Payton ran toward his horse.

Aunt Vi laughed. "Sometimes it seems as if that boy is already sowing his wild oats."

"It seems so cruel . . . to the boy horses," said Maya.

"Oh, it's not much different in human families. There comes a time when children must leave home and find their own way in the world. Like your mother did, like you and Payton will do someday. As heart-wrenching as it seems, in a few years, Klee will be sent away from the band, too."

Maya and Aunt Vi lifted their binoculars. Maya watched as Artemisia nibbled Klee's neck and then wrapped her large head and neck around his body. Maya felt a pang of jealousy. Had her mother ever cuddled her with such devotion?

"She's a good mother," said Aunt Vi. "And a good lead mare. As much as I miss her, I can tell she's happy."

"How did Artemisia get to be the lead mare?" asked Maya.

"The mare who puts herself in the position of leader becomes it," said Aunt Vi.

"But how did Artemisia *know* she was the leader?"

"Oh, Maya, there's so much we humans don't know about 'knowing.' With horses, it's not the biggest or oldest who is the lead. It's the horse who has the confidence to guide the family in times of danger, who has knowledge of the land and knows the routes to safety, who is herd-smart and can make alliances with other mares and keep peace. Some mares have the ability. Others don't. Think about great human leaders. They have many of those same qualities."

Maya thought about what Aunt Vi had just said and lowered her binoculars. "Like you, Aunt Vi."

Aunt Vi continued to watch the horses for a few moments, then set the binoculars aside and swiped her forearm across her eyes. "Maya . . . remember how I told you about how much your mother loved the Sweetwater and how it filled up her heart like no other place could?"

Maya nodded and turned to look at Aunt Vi, whose eyes shined a little too bright.

"I never married or had a family of my own . . . and your mother . . . filled up a place in my heart that I didn't think could be filled up ever again . . . until . . ."

Payton appeared behind them, holding all three horses by their reins, breathless and panting. "Aunt Vi!"

She smiled at Maya. "Guess he saved me from falling into the mush pot. What is it, Payton?"

"Aunt Vi . . . there's a 'copter . . . in the canyon!"

Aunt Vi sucked in air, and her face crumpled with disappointment. "No!"

"What's happening?" asked Maya.

"Come on!" said Payton. "Hurry."

Aunt Vi hastened toward the horses, and Maya ran after her. As they mounted, Aunt Vi said, "At least you got to see them . . . before . . ."

Maya demanded, "Before what?"

The clapping of helicopter blades and the buzz of a motor intensified. The machine appeared on the horizon, swooping and zigzagging like a giant bumblebee across the wide canyon. Miles of net fencing had been set up as a trap, wider at one end of the canyon than at the other, funneling into a narrow chute and ending in a large circular holding pen.

Wild horses pounded forward, panicked and snorting. Their coats glistened with sweat. A young filly hurried to keep up with her mother. A stallion stumbled and was jostled forward with the stampeding throng. A mare struggled behind, lame. Horse screams echoed in the canyon.

Maya, Payton, and Aunt Vi sat on a ridge and watched. "It's a gather, but it's not pretty, is it?"

Maya shook her head. The word *gather* sounded so gentle. But there was nothing gentle about this. "Why are they taking them?"

"Many reasons and it's complicated. The government rounds them up every few years to keep the wild horse population under control. And there's a lot of pressure on them to keep doing just that, whether it's necessary or not. Some ranchers think they damage the grazing land for their cattle. Some people think they drink too much water. But there's a counter-argument for all of those opinions. Others say they're just feral horses, broomtails, left over from old ranches and domesticated stock, that have learned to survive in the wild. Some may be, but now there are scientists who believe that mustangs are a wild species native to North America. Regardless of their origin, there are many people who wish they were more protected."

"What's going to happen to them?"

"The prettiest and youngest will get purchased at auctions, like the one where I adopted Artemisia. Others will be bought by people who work for sanctuaries, protected places where they can live peacefully in freedom."

"But there's plenty of land here, and they're already free," said Maya.

"That's a point that is often made. Unfortunately,

we've done this many times in our country, rounded up people or animals and released them someplace else when they were just fine where they were."

"What happens to the others . . . the leftovers?"

Payton lowered his binoculars and seemed eerily calm. "They auction them off and lots of them are bought and killed for their meat. Then they ship it to other countries. They used to sell the horses to slaughter-houses to make dog food out of them."

"The law to protect the horses is often challenged by legislators to satisfy certain voters whose livestock graze on the public land," said Aunt Vi. "Wild horses eat grass and don't make money for anyone. Their value is not understood by everybody. Yet this country was born on the backs of horses. Horses moved people from place to place so the country could be developed. They tilled the land and became our trusted mounts and allies in war. As a species, they reached out to us as much as we did to them. They became our companions. See how alive they are and filled with energy and abandon? In a matter of days, if we return to this holding pen, you'll see how dispirited they've become. Imagine being free and then separated from your family and put in confinement."

Maya didn't have to imagine. Her emotions stirred. She looked out at the infinite and unpopulated landscape and ached for the horses. Artemisia had once been separated from her own mother during a gather. Now she might lose Klee in the same way.

Aunt Vi's binoculars swept back and forth across

the string of horses. "There's Sargent . . . Georgia and Mary . . . and even Wyeth. He must have been trailing after them."

The rope-waving mustangers rode abreast behind the last of the captured horses until the holding pen gate was slammed shut.

"What about Artemisia and Klee?" asked Maya.

Aunt Vi continued to study the confused and anxious horses, milling in the corral. "They're missing."

Maya blew out a sigh of relief. "That's good, right?"

Aunt Vi put her binoculars in her saddlebag. Her forehead creased with apprehension. "Maybe. Maybe not. If they'd been captured, Maya, I would have had the chance to prove that Artemisia belongs to me. She still carries the ranch brand. But now . . . without the protection of a stallion, she and Klee are vulnerable. . . ."

"What could happen to them?" asked Maya.

Aunt Vi looked at her in a way that told her the unimaginable could happen.

They didn't talk on the ride back to the trailer. Or in the truck on the way back to camp. Payton slumped against the passenger door. Aunt Vi stared straight ahead at the road. Maya leaned her head back against the seat and closed her eyes. She could not stop thinking about Artemisia and Klee, nor could she squash her overwhelming desire to get on a horse and ride out to find them.

18

ARTEMISIA KNEW WHAT THE SOUND OF THE REPETITIVE

thwapping meant. It meant to run with panic within a frantic

throng. It meant bloodied cannons from the crush of hooves, and

lather so thick from exertion that it flung into one another's

eyes.

Artemisia's instincts had told her that Klee could not sur-

vive the fury, so she had veered away from the cloud of dust and

the swath of ground that had been trampled smooth by hun-

dreds of thundering hooves.

They had been on their own for several days now, wandering

north of the gulch toward the Sweetwater River. It was almost

dark. A sage grouse flew from a clump of brush. Artemisia

lifted her head in the direction of the rustle, her ears contorting to determine the cause. The wind shifted and she smelled the mountain lion. Artemisia kept close to Klee. With her foal at her side, she galloped toward open land where she would have a chance against an attack. The mountain lion would be alone; it was a solitary creature with no need for companionship. In wide-open space, Artemisia might be able to stave off a single predator.

Once, from a high ridge, she had watched a mountain lion stalk and kill a pronghorn. The huge cat had stayed downwind and well hidden in the brushy foothills. With its tawny belly close to the ground, it sleuthed forward. Then, it waited, patient and quiet, in the sagebrush. As the intended prey drifted closer, the cat's black-tipped ears twitched and its back swayed. It squatted onto its powerful hind legs and leaped twenty feet to the pronghorn's back. With one vicious bite on the neck, it immobilized and killed the victim. After satisfying its hunger, the mountain lion covered what was left of the carcass with dirt and leaves to be revisited for future meals.

Now, the scent grew stronger. A shadow shifted, and Artemisia saw the crouching lion. Her ears flattened and her nostrils flared. She clamped down her tail and squealed a terrifying warning. The cat sprang, and Artemisia felt the eerie, tingling sensation of something swooshing toward her. She reared and met the attacker with pummeling hooves.

The surprised cat fled.

Artemisia huddled close to Klee. With swift determination, she chose a path and led him away. They needed to leave the area.

The mountain lion was hungry and it would stalk them again and again, until it was successful.

19

Maya and Payton heard the distinctive throttle of Moose's truck and raced from the river, side by side, to the campsite. Already free of the cab, Golly bounded toward the two cousins, pouncing at their feet, barking and licking their outstretched hands.

Moose and Fig climbed from the cab and moseyed forward. Moose gave Maya a side-arm hug. "Well, now, how's the frontier girl?"

Her words spewed. "We saw the wild horses. There was a roundup, but it's really called a gather, and Artemisia and Klee . . . Oh, Klee is Artemisia's new foal. . . . Well, they're missing. We looked for them all day yesterday but couldn't find them in their usual places. Aunt Vi said they could be anywhere, but we're determined to keep looking. And guess what? I can lope, really fast."

"Of course you can," said Uncle Fig as he held Payton under his arm in a headlock and tousled his hair.

"C'mon, Golly," said Payton, breaking free. "I'll show you the beaver dam near Maya's tepee."

He ran toward the river and the dog followed, but Maya stayed back.

Aunt Vi emerged from the office tent, greeted Fig and Moose, and with her usual sense of urgency, passed supplies from the bed of the truck to any willing hands. Maya accepted a bag of groceries and walked alongside them toward the campsite.

"Is this the same girl we left out here a few weeks back?" asked Moose.

Maya smiled and nodded.

"Can't be," said Fig. "This girl is a little taller, got more color in her face, and can lope really fast."

"You two stop pestering," said Aunt Vi. "Part of her is new and part of her is the same. Once I got her on a horse, she found her heart, just like her mother."

They dropped off the bags in the pantry and headed back to the truck for another load.

"So the story you told us about the horses . . . that true, Maya?" asked Moose.

"Yes. I'm not lying, am I, Aunt Vi?"

"You can believe every word she says these days."

"Vi, you think Artemisia and her colt could be along the river?" asked Fig.

They paused over the truck bed.

"I don't know," said Aunt Vi. "I'm not sure why they weren't with the herd during the gather. Since Artemisia was captured once before, maybe she shied at the sound of the helicopter. Months ago, I saw her band at a clearing near the river a few times, which was an odd place for them to be since it's so far from their usual range. Artemisia might migrate back there out of habit. Or she might go someplace completely different if she felt threatened."

"Aunt Vi says that it would be hard for them to survive without the protection of a stallion," said Maya, her voice sounding forlorn and desperate. "But now there's not that many stallions because of the gather. And horses want to be around other horses. And one of the saddest things on earth is a wild horse without a family. They just wander around, sad and lonely . . . until maybe something bad happens."

"Well, then, we'd better get them back, Maya-bird,"

said Moose, handing her another bag of groceries. He turned to Aunt Vi. "That horse is branded and rightfully yours."

"I know. If they've been taken into another band," said Aunt Vi, "I'll leave them in the wild. But if they're struggling on their own, I'd sure like to bring them here."

"Yes . . . we'd like to bring them here," repeated Maya. "Can we go looking for them after lunch?" she asked. "Please?"

Moose looked toward The Winds and pointed. "We can . . . unless that weather catches up to us."

Veiled fingers of purple and black descended from the sky. The rain pelted. Clouds flashed and tossed thunderous accusations back and forth. The plastic chairs around the campfire were moved into the kitchen tent where the campers hunkered together. Moose and Fig dashed out to feed the horses and dig trenches to redirect encroaching puddles.

After two days of intermittent downpours, and what seemed like hundreds of card games with Payton, listening for hours to Moose read from a Louis L'Amour novel, and Uncle Fig's lessons on the Latin names of the flora and fauna of Wyoming, Maya tired of the kitchen tent.

She poked her head into the field office, where Aunt Vi was catching up on her work. "Can I come in?"

"Be my guest. I was wondering how long you'd last in there with the boys."

Maya looked around at the haphazard untidiness. Aunt Vi sat on a folding chair at the desk. Slick-covered horse magazines littered the floor. On the canvas walls, Aunt Vi had pinned an array of photographs of the wild horses, with their names scrawled across the borders.   •

"You need any help?" asked Maya.

"Make any amount of order out of this chaos and I'll be grateful. I'd love to have those boxes unpacked. I'm working on an article called 'The Native Horse Through the Artist's Eye' for a journal, and then I need to start on my fall lesson plans for my art history classes."

Lightning flashed and illuminated the tent. Maya held her breath until the thunder crashed around them.

Aunt Vi continued to work, unconcerned.

Maya took a deep breath and began to unpack the boxes, taking out oversize art books, one by one, smoothing her hand across each cover: John Singer Sargent, Artemisia Gentileschi, Olaf Seltzer, George Catlin, Charles Russell, N. C. Wyeth, Mary Cassatt. . . .

Maya smiled and examined the photos of the wild horses pinned to the walls of the tent, matching them with the corresponding art books. She studied a photo of a black stallion with a white blaze and white stockings. "Aunt Vi, this looks like the horse my father painted."

"You're right. That's Remington. Isn't he magnificent? He's tried to steal Artemisia from Sargent's band a few times but has never succeeded. Horses have their own personalities, their own ways to get what they want."

"Like people?" asked Maya.

"It's more the other way around. People are like horses. Sargent is more of a warrior. He doesn't hesitate to fight to get what he wants. Remington would protect his own, but his approach to getting his way is different. He's a patient opportunist, waiting until a stallion drops his guard before moving in. I still see Remington, racing along the top of a ridge with a few bachelors. He doesn't have a mare yet. It would be nice if he was still pining for Artemisia. She and Klee could use the protection." Aunt Vi stood and stretched. "I'm going to make a sandwich. You hungry?"

Maya shook her head. She stacked the magazines into neat piles, with their spines all facing the same direction. She aligned the books alphabetically and straightened the reports and papers. There was something satisfying in putting it all to order for Aunt Vi, and Maya found herself humming.

While sorting a stack of files, she came across a tattered envelope of photos. The contents caused her to stop and sink cross-legged to the ground. She laid the series of photographs in a line: Maya's mother with Aunt

Vi in front of a split-rail fence, their arms around each other; a four-year-old Maya holding Moose's hand and walking in the pasture; Maya and Payton on Fig's lap in a porch rocker; her mother riding Artemisia bareback, with nothing more than a rope around the horse's barrel. And a duplicate of the photo Maya had in her shoe box.

Maya gathered the pictures, tucked them inside her jacket, and dashed through the rain and mud to the kitchen tent. She found Moose reading and Uncle Fig and Payton playing checkers.

She handed the photographs to Moose. "What's that rope on Artemisia?"

He studied the photo. "Maya-bird, I'd forgotten about that. We called it a Comanche Coil. Tribes of the Great Plains Indians used this technique to ride without a saddle or reins. They wrapped a rope around the horse in a giant belly loop, sat bareback, and tucked their knees under the rope on either side. They held on by slipping a hand underneath the rope where it crossed the withers. The American Indians were such great horsemen that they could hunt and fight wars from that position."

Fig looked up from the checkers game. "We told your mother about the belly loop and she couldn't rest until she tried it. Ellie was fearless."

"Like me?" asked Payton.

"No," said Fig, grinning. "You're fearless like a bull in a china shop. Ellie was fearless but kept her wits about her. She always wanted to try something new but she thought about it carefully before she did it."

Maya leaned on Moose's arm as he flipped through

the photographs. He reached the one of her mother on Artemisia, laughing and waving. "I remember this. Know who your mom was smiling and waving at?"

Maya shook her head.

"It was you," said Moose. "I was holding you in my arms and a hawk flew overhead, round and round in circles. You burst out in a fit of giggles, pointing to the sky. Ellie was so tickled with your reaction that she started laughing out loud, too, and Aunt Vi took the picture."

Maya stared at the photo. Her mother had been waving to *her*? *She* had been the one to make her mother so happy? A kernel of contentment planted itself in her mind. She slid away from Moose's side and pulled back the window flap on the tent. Showers swept across the campsite, but she looked beyond the curtains of water. She could already imagine Artemisia and Klee in the corral. She would feed them and pet them. She would talk to them, too, and tell them a thousand little things. She even imagined herself riding Artemisia, like her mother had.

"When can we look for Artemisia and Klee?" she asked.

"As soon as this rain lets up, Maya," said Moose. "And I hope it stops soon or we'll all be in the river."

The earth sopped up the relentless water from the clouds, and the river brimmed with renewed energy. Mornings brought more riding lessons and sometimes fishing with Fig and Moose. Afternoons, Aunt Vi, Maya, and Payton took long rides to search for Artemisia and Klee. They rode for miles on one of the California pioneer trails. They paralleled an old railroad grade. They trailered to the Elkhorn Draw and back out to the Honeycomb Buttes. At first, when they arrived back in camp without news, they remained optimistic. But after several weeks, they returned from their searches quiet and pensive.

Payton stopped going with them, preferring to stay at camp with Fig and Moose. Aunt Vi told Maya they needed to take a break from the long rides so she could catch up on her work and give the horses a rest. But Maya didn't give up hope. Every night before she went to sleep, she took out the little black stallion, swept it above her head, and whispered, "Don't worry, Artemisia. I am coming for you."

Gallop

20

MAYA CARRIED AN ARMLOAD OF WOOD THROUGH THE willows, savoring the morning sounds of the camp on the Sweetwater: the flitting and trills of the sage thrasher, the soft clatters of someone in the kitchen tent, the gurgle of the percolator on the fire, and the occasional subdued whinny that drifted down from the corrals. Until she heard crying.

She dropped the wood and ran to the campsite, where she found Payton in one of the chairs, slumped over and moaning with pain. Blood oozed from his mouth. Aunt Vi stood over him with a wad of tissues, blotting the bleeding.

"You were running backward again, weren't you?" said Aunt Vi.

He nodded.

"And tripped over your own feet?"

He nodded.

"Maya, find me the truck keys. He knocked out a tooth, and I need to get him to the dentist. I'd feel a lot better if you came with me, but I understand if you don't want to drive all the way to town to spend the day in a dentist's office."

"I'll be fine," said Maya. "I'll finish stacking wood and sweep out the tents and then I'll read until Moose and Fig get back."

"Okay, I trust you to do just that. They will be back late this afternoon from Tack and Feed with a load of hay. Tell them what happened and that I don't know how long this will take with Payton. We might have to stay overnight back home at the ranch. In which case

Payton will get to see the Fourth of July parade in town."

"Yes!" he said through the wad of tissues over his mouth.

"Maya, I'll see you later today or first thing in the morning." Aunt Vi never stopped talking as Maya helped Payton into the truck. "Don't go in the river. We've had more rain than usual and the pools are deep. You can gather kindling if you like but don't light a fire until someone's here. Keep the horses in the corral and you stay put."

"I will." She rushed to the passenger window. "Payton, I hope you feel better."

When the truck pulled away, Maya walked back to the campsite. It was the first time she had ever been at camp by herself, and she felt proud that Aunt Vi had trusted her. She followed her plan, point by point, stacking wood and sweeping out the tents. When she finally opened the flap to her tepee, she drew in her breath.

Centered on her pillow lay the little brown-and-white horse that Payton had thrown into the bushes. She picked up the figure and cradled it in the palms of her hands. How had he ever found it? It must have taken him forever to search through the willows. And when had Payton sneaked inside her tepee to leave it for her? Had he been running away from her tent when he fell and hurt himself? She put it in the pocket of her vest and zipped it tight. As she swept, she paused every few moments to pat her pocket, and wondered what she could do for Payton in return.

Later, Maya sat near the fire pit, flipping through one of Aunt Vi's art magazines, when a golden eagle distracted her. The bird of prey floated over the campsite, its wings outstretched in a fan of feathers. Payton collected feathers! Maybe if she could determine the location of the bird's aerie, she could find a feather on the ground below. When the eagle glided toward a rock ledge down-river, she grabbed the binoculars and hiked to the top of the outcropping above her tepee. There, she had a panoramic view for miles. She glassed until a flash of white caught her eye. Carefully, she panned the binoculars and refocused the lens to find the eagle. Her breath caught.

Artemisia!

The horse stood on the other side of the gorge, down-river in the cradle of two mountains. Above her, an aspen grove peppered the hillsides. Below, a grass meadow met the river. Maya lowered the binoculars and looked at camp and then back toward the horse. Distances were often deceiving out here, and Artemisia was probably much farther away than she appeared. How long would it take to reach her? she wondered.

Maya and Aunt Vi had crossed the gorge on horseback last week, by traversing down the mountain and fording the river. That alone had taken well over an hour of careful maneuvering. And Artemisia was much farther away. Even if Maya were able to reach Artemisia and Klee, then what?

Maya remembered her promise to Aunt Vi. She should sit tight and hope the horse was still there when someone came back. But that might be hours from now. Suppose Artemisia left? And where was Klee? Would it be so wrong to check on them? Aunt Vi would do the same if she had the chance. She'd understand. Maybe Maya could entice Artemisia and Klee in this direction. Lure them into camp. Aunt Vi would be so surprised . . . and grateful.

Maya turned toward the corrals and saw the blue plastic container of molasses grain. A wild horse who'd never tasted the grain might not be interested, but Artemisia had been a remuda horse and would have developed a taste for the sweet food. Aunt Vi sometimes gave the horses apples for a treat, so Artemisia might have a taste for them, too. The prospect of seeing Artemisia up close possessed Maya. She peered through the binoculars again and remembered Aunt Vi's words. *Ellie adored that horse and rode her the entire time she was here. Artemisia and your mother had a connection like I've never seen before. When Ellie left, Artemisia pined for days.*

"My mother loved you," whispered Maya. "And you loved her."

Maya glanced at her clothes. She already wore a long-sleeved shirt and her vest, but she had learned that the weather was unpredictable. She ran to her tepee and grabbed her mother's jacket, then rushed back to the corrals to tack Seltzer. She tied the jacket behind the saddle, hung the binoculars around her neck, filled a canvas drawstring bag with the molasses grain and three apples, and slung it over the saddle horn. She grabbed a halter from the tack bench and stuffed it in the saddle bag. Klee wouldn't need a halter because if Maya could halter Artemisia, the foal would follow. Maya mounted Seltzer and headed up the road, away from camp.

She paused at the top of the gorge. "Okay, boy, nice and slow." She walked Seltzer down the escarpment sideways in a wide zigzag pattern, giving him plenty of reins so he could drop his head and pick among the woody sage and rocks. The river lay below in swirling eddies and engorged pools. Sunlight disappeared in the shadow of the cliff face, and the dimness gave an ominous and foreboding feeling to the long descent.

Still in the saddle, Maya rested at the river's edge and allowed Seltzer to drink. In the shade of the mountain, the air had grown chilly. Maya untied her jacket and put it on, then crossed in the shallows to the other bank. She and the horse penetrated through the robe of deep greenery and continued parallel to the river.

How long had she been gone? she wondered. It felt like several hours, but she'd discovered that on trail rides away from camp, time played games.

Maya and Seltzer continued, making slow passage above the willow line. The afternoon light diminished. "Just a little farther, boy. Otherwise, we won't be able to get back before dark." She skirted a large rocky prominence. As she turned into yet another river cove, she spotted Artemisia, who stood patient and statuesque, halfway up the slope, as if waiting for someone. Maya's throat tightened and her eyes moistened. "Are you waiting for me? I'm coming, Artemisia."

She turned Seltzer into the grass meadow that stretched upward toward the aspens. With slow and measured steps, the horse maneuvered over trees that had been felled by snow in winter and now lay dead. As Maya and Seltzer approached, Artemisia backed into the higher reaches of the grove.

"Hey, girl. I'm . . . Maya. Don't run away. Do you remember my mother . . . Ellie?"

Artemisia took several skittish steps to the side and back.

"What's the matter, girl?" Maya dismounted and slung Seltzer's reins over a branch. She scanned through the trees. A wisp of wind tickled the leaves of the quaking aspens and the entire grove shuddered.

Populus tremuloides, Maya thought, remembering Uncle Fig's lessons.

Artemisia nickered.

"You're even more beautiful up close, Artemisia. Where's Klee? Where's your baby?" Her eyes slowly scanned one side of the grove, and then she turned toward the ledge of rock that bordered the other side. Her eyes fastened on a mass of brown-and-white hair lying motionless and silent. Maya shivered.

She treaded forward, taking small hesitant steps, trying to stave the awful possibilities from her mind. Moving closer, she saw the dreaded paw tracks of a mountain lion.

Klee's young body lay mangled and bloodied. Leaves and dirt half covered the sweet face in the cat's frugal attempt to hide the kill. The smell of the desecration fouled the air. Maya's stomach recoiled. She leaned against a tree, doubled over, and vomited. When she righted herself, tears stung her eyes.

Maya backed away from Klee and turned toward Artemisia.

The horse stared at the girl, then dropped her large head.

Maya put a hand over her heart and felt a sickening ache inside. "Your baby . . ." She sat for a long while, watching Artemisia's aimless meanderings at the back of the grove. First, she had lost the protection of her family, and now she'd lost her foal. Maya couldn't leave her alone to suffer the same fate as Klee.

Maya knew she should start back to camp. She lifted into the saddle and removed the canvas bag from the horn. She slung the drawstring over a shoulder, pulled the bag into her lap, and opened it enough to reach a hand inside. She turned Seltzer toward the river, dropped a handful of food, moved a few feet forward, and paused to woo Artemisia. "Come on. Everything will be okay. Come with me now."

Seltzer nickered, as if he knew that reassurance was necessary, and Artemisia answered. Did she recognize Seltzer from the remuda years before? Or was her desire for companionship so strong that any living voice soothed her longing? For whatever reason, Artemisia inched forward.

Maya didn't take her eyes from Artemisia. She could see why her mother had loved her. There was something thrilling about the pulse in her nicker and the righteous way she held her head and tossed her mane. And yet, there was a sense of vulnerability about her, too, as if her eyes asked permission to be saved and loved.

Maya looked at the sun. She needed to hurry so she could get back. If Aunt Vi and Payton decided to return to camp, they would be worried when Maya wasn't there. "Follow me, Artemisia," she called.

The little caravan neared the bank of the river.

Suddenly agitated, Seltzer danced in a circle and whinnied. Maya settled him and looked around but could see nothing that would have made him shy. A moment later, a sage grouse whisked from a bush. A family of cottontails darted out of hiding and seemed confused as to where to run. Magpies erupted from the aspen trees with rapid *yak-yak-yak*-ing, and a beaver emerged from a hole in the bank and quickly slid into the water. Maya glanced back at Artemisia, who stood with her neck arched, ears back, pawing at the ground.

Maya stroked Seltzer's neck. She took a deep breath and tried to quell the anxious feeling inside of her. Who or what had made the animals feel threatened?

21

THE GROUND QUAVERED. SELTZER STUMBLED AND MAYA hurtled from his back. She tried to grab the leather skirt of the saddle to steady herself, but the earth twisted again and she fell facedown. The heavy binoculars jabbed her chest, and the bag of grain thumped her back. Rocks tumbled into the meadow from the ridge above. Artemisia squealed. The shaking persisted as Maya dug her nails into the wavering earth.

When the temblor stopped, she forced herself to breathe. Seltzer had snagged his reins in a bush and strained against them, screaming with distress. Maya called to him, "Whoa, boy. Whoa . . ."

Seltzer paused, his eyes bulging. He reared and the

reins snapped from the bush. In a frenzied gallop, he disappeared uphill.

"Seltzer! Seltzer!" Maya started after him, until she heard a noise like the roar of an approaching train behind her. She turned toward the Sweetwater.

Downstream, the mountain across the river descended in a mammoth slide of rock and dirt. The rush of earth propelled trees, boulders, and all manner of debris toward the river. The deafening noise increased and the force of the wind quivered as it approached. As strong as a hurricane, the rush lifted Maya from the ground and for a moment, she had the sensation of flying. She landed on her back and felt her breath *whoosh* from her body. She lay motionless until her lungs refilled. As she rolled onto her hands and knees, she felt her heart thrashing.

Artemisia had been thrust to the ground. Maya

spotted her nearby, enveloped within a tangle of aspen limbs and logs. The horse's heart, too, bulged rapidly in and out. Maya crawled closer. "There, girl. There. We're okay."

The horse struggled but could not uplift the pile. Maya scooted above Artemisia's head and tugged at the logs and branches, but the horse was buried.

The Sweetwater had been dammed by the slide and now the water crept upward toward them. Maya stood and heaved a large branch from Artemisia, then another, and another. At the same time, a matted jungle of rubble rushed downriver, creating a surge of water that splashed over Artemisia's hooves.

"Come on, Artemisia!" Maya tugged at the end of a branch and flung it aside. She pulled the timber from the pile, piece by piece.

Artemisia struggled to rise, but two large logs still crossed and pinned her.

Maya heaved the end of one and flung it aside, surprised by her own strength.

At last, the mare lifted her head and neck, and rolled over, the remaining log cascading from her back. She jerked upward and stood.

Maya backed into the grove. "Come on, girl. This way!"

The horse took a few wobbly steps toward Maya.

Another gush from the river pushed a roiling swath of water toward them. Maya jumped backward, but it curled around Artemisia's legs. The horse stumbled and tried to scramble upward but fell in the slosh, squealing.

"You can do it!" called Maya. "Come on!"

Artemisia stood again. Dirt that had not had a chance

to turn to mud stuck to her coat. As Artemisia staggered after Maya higher into the aspen grove, an aftershock strummed. The horse fell to the ground on her side and began sliding downhill.

Maya lunged toward a tree trunk to steady herself and heard rubble sliding from the hillside above. She spun around to see a waterfall of rocks descending on Klee, entombing him. The ground swayed again. Maya tried to stay upright but another sudden jolt sent her somersaulting downward in a merry-go-round of earth and sky. She plunged into a rock face.

Maya moaned. Pain riddled her right foot and arm and her head throbbed. She opened her eyes, but everything blurred. Blinking, she tried to make sense of the shadows above her. Was she staring at the ceiling in her room at Grandmother's house?

She took a deep breath, squinted, and tried to focus. The shadows became a blur of green, and then the blur became leaves silhouetted against the late afternoon sun. But where was she? Her mind wrestled. Seltzer. The river. The aspen grove . . .

Artemisia! What had happened to her? Maya tried to sit up but abandoned the attempt. She felt too woozy and nauseous. Lifting and twisting the sore arm, she saw that her jacket and shirt had been ripped from the shoulder to the elbow. Underneath, a wide gash leaked blood onto her clothing. The shadows spun. "Artemisia . . ." she murmured, a moment before she saw a bouquet of tiny pinpoints of light. Then everything faded to black.

Persistent nudging and a low, throaty nicker roused Maya. She squinted at blurry white blotches. Someone hovered. She blinked and opened her eyes wider.

Artemisia stood above her. The horse's head dropped close to Maya's body, the mane tickling her neck. The sun had almost disappeared, and the river lapped at Maya's boots. She reached for Artemisia's dangling mane but the horse backed away, just out of her grasp. Maya rolled to her stomach and pulled herself to her hands and knees. Needles of pain jabbed at her right foot and the boot felt much too tight. She whimpered. A wave of dizziness followed and she retched.

Artemisia nickered at her again, as if insisting she move.

Maya crawled to a tree, raised herself against the trunk, and huddled next to it until her nausea subsided.

247

Artemisia walked farther into the grove, paused, and turned to look at Maya.

"I'm coming," said Maya. She gazed uphill, befuddled. Something was wrong. She studied the scene until she knew. Every tree had been defoliated from the blast of wind, and the entire vale was now carpeted with leaves. The naked white trunks of the aspens looked like candles placed haphazardly on the side of a lopsided cake. The grassy area closest to the river looked swept clean. Farther up the vale, the leaves had resettled in dunes of foliage.

Maya took tiny hops, tree to tree, up the slope on her good leg until she found a shallow depression between several trunks. She dropped to the ground, pushing leaves and duff into a soft mattress, then positioned herself on top of it.

She slipped off the canvas bag and the binoculars and then struggled to remove her right boot. It would not budge, and the pain was too intense to keep trying. Shivering, she lifted the hood of the jacket over her head and scooped more leaves across her legs for warmth. The sky grew darker.

"Artemisia," Maya called. "Please stay with me. . . ." She scanned the grove but didn't see her. She reached inside her jacket, unzipped the pocket of her vest, and pulled out the small brown-and-white Paint. "Where did you go?" Maya strained to hear a friendly nicker, but there was no response.

Instead, she heard a rustling and cringed. She grabbed a nearby branch and slapped the leaves near her legs to dissuade the voles and mice. She lay back and wished for a tepee with a zipper.

22

Maya's throbbing foot woke her in the gray window before sunrise.

The sky was still ashen, the grove silent. She sat up, her eyes darting through the trees until she spotted Artemisia on the hillside, browsing. "There you are. . . . You stayed. . . ."

Artemisia lifted her head, looked in Maya's direction, and then continued foraging for grass.

Pain overshadowed Maya's relief. Her right foot felt as if it were in a vise, and the wound on her arm now oozed pink syrup. She knew it needed to be cleaned, but she ached with cold, and the river water would be freezing this early in the morning. She pulled more leaves onto her lap and lay back, watching the sky brighten. A flood of worry overtook her. What had happened to Aunt Vi and Payton? Where had they been during the earthquake? Had they made it to the ranch? And Moose and Fig? Had they been at camp or pulling a trailer-load of hay? They might have gone off the road or crashed. Or maybe something worse had happened. She cringed at the idea. What about Seltzer and Golly? Had they survived? And what did they all think had happened to her?

The sun climbed higher and the morning warmed. Maya fashioned a cane from a branch and shuffled to the river where she lowered herself for a long drink of water. Sitting on a log, she took off her jacket, vest, and shirt, peeling the fabric away from the arm wound and wincing when it stuck to her skin. She took off the left boot and sock and pulled her left leg out of her jeans. Still wearing the right leg of her jeans and the right boot and sock, she lowered herself into a shallow pool that was surrounded by a natural rock dam. The boot flooded. Cold, soothing water reached her toes, easing the pain in her foot. Maya allowed it to soak.

She watched as Artemisia made her way to the river. Instead of her usual gracefulness, the mare walked with a sluggish and stiff gait. She stopped at the edge of the river, not twenty feet from Maya, and drank.

"You must be bruised and sore, too. We both need to get better, Artemisia. But first, I have to get this boot off because it's much too tight. . . ." Holding the heel and toe, Maya tugged and the right boot released with a slurp. She yelled out with pain.

Artemisia's ears twisted at Maya's cry.

Maya gently pulled her wet jeans from her right leg

and then stripped off the sock. At the sight of the grotesquely bruised and disjointed ankle, she felt sick again. Taking deep breaths, she willed her stomach to settle. "It's worse . . . than I thought. It's clearly broken." Released from the confines of the boot, the ankle ballooned. "Maybe taking off my boot wasn't such a good idea. . . ."

Artemisia plodded back into the grove.

Maya called after her, "Please don't go far." She submerged the arm wound. The sting made her suck in her breath through clenched teeth. She doused her arm several times, then rinsed her clothes in the river, too.

After dragging herself back to the aspens, Maya spread out her clothes to dry in the early afternoon sun and sat on a rock.

"Look at me, Artemisia. I'm sitting here in public

in my underwear. I guess we're not actually in public but we're in the middle of . . . somewhere. Grandmother would have found this incredibly inappropriate."

Artemisia kept her usual distance but raised her head toward Maya and continued chewing.

Maya noticed that Artemisia looked at her or came closer at the sound of her voice. "Nobody even knows where I am, except you, Artemisia. Do you think they'll come looking for me? I hope they do . . . because I can't walk. If they don't come, would you let me ride you out of here? I need you to trust me, Artemisia . . . so I can get home . . . if they don't come."

Artemisia took one step in her direction, but no farther.

Maya sighed. Anchoring one corner of the kerchief

in her teeth, she wrapped the cloth snugly around the gash in her arm and secured it. When her clothes were dry, she dressed. While it was still light, Maya ate one of the apples, then put out a handful of the molasses grain for Artemisia. The aspen grove had plenty of grass, but Maya hoped the horse would be tempted by the delicacy and come even closer.

Maya zipped her jacket, tied the hood snug, and burrowed into the leaves. Weary, she lay back and watched the sky fade. She remembered the first day she had arrived at camp and Aunt Vi had said, "Don't let that sky swallow you up."

Could it really do that? Could she just vanish? she wondered. A lone white dot appeared. Then another. And another. The heavens unfolded and the Milky Way emerged as a bright smear across the night drapery. The stars were so dense that the darkness barely peeked through the brightness. Maya gazed at the immense sky, spellbound. *How will anyone ever find me?*

In the morning, the molasses grain Maya had put out the night before had disappeared and Artemisia browsed a little closer to Maya's nest. As Maya took slow, painful steps to the river to rinse her arm and soak her ankle, Artemisia relocated along with her, staying near but too far away to touch.

The pool in which Maya had bathed yesterday was deeper now and the rocks surrounding it were almost submerged. Two small trout swam in the well, pushed in by a surge of water overnight and now trapped. The pool was smaller than a bathtub and she could easily stand in it and use her vest as a scoop to flip the fish onto the shore. But then how would she cook it? Hunger grabbed at her stomach. She left the trout in their holding pen, found another spot in which to soak, and thought about the possibility of fire.

Back beneath the aspens, Maya unscrewed a lens from the binoculars. She cleared an area of debris, built a rock circle, and fashioned a pile of tiny twigs over a mound of leaves. She'd seen the boys across the street from Grandmother's burn leaves with a magnifying glass. Would this work? Maya angled the lens until a bright dot appeared on the tinder. How long would it take to capture the sun? Within seconds, a hair of smoke drifted upward. Excited, she moved her hand slightly and the smoking stopped. She repositioned the lens and a thin, cloudy line lifted again. For an hour she made tiny trails of smoke but no flames.

Her stomach cramped at the possibility of fish for dinner. At last, an orange ember glowed. She dared not move the lens and willed a flame to appear. "Come on," she whispered, but the kindling refused to ignite.

After dozens of attempts, Maya's resolve crumbled. Frustrated, she gave up on the fire and ate the second apple. But she wasn't satisified, so she ate the last one, too. As the night sky presented another show of studded beauty, she put a handful of molasses grain on the ground not far from her feet.

This time, Artemisia didn't wait until Maya was asleep to walk over and nibble at it. Maya talked to her in a slow, gentle voice. "Do you know that song? The one about the stars? I used to sing it when I was little. 'Twinkle, twinkle, little star . . .'"

Softly, Artemisia nickered.

"You're absolutely right, Artemisia. I sang it wrong.
It goes like this:

Ellie, Ellie, Ellie, Ellie . . .

Ellie, Ellie, Ellie, Ellie . . ."

23

In the morning, Maya unburied herself from her coverlet of leaves and called out to Artemisia. "Are you there, girl?"

She sat up and spied the horse ambling toward the river. Relieved, she brushed the leaves from her clothes. "I've been gone for three nights, Artemisia, and no one has come to find me. Do you think they think I'm . . . dead?" Before she could bemoan her situation, a high-pitched whining distracted her. She swatted at a mosquito and then another, but it did no good. Swarms seemed to have hatched overnight. She tied the hood of her jacket around her face, but they found her hands, the injured foot, which was still too swollen for a sock, and the tender parts of her cheeks.

She scooted to the river, where she found Artemisia rolling in the water, legs in the air. The horse emerged on the bank and wallowed in the dirt and grass. When she stood, she looked breaded, like a chicken cutlet.

"I know, I know. That's how you keep the bugs and flies away. I'll try anything." After rinsing in the river, Maya ensconced herself in her jacket again and dabbed a thick coat of mud on her cheeks, the tops of her hands, and the foot. The mud helped, but the mosquitoes still darted around her, singing their high-pitched songs. They even tried to bite through her jeans. Miserable, she huddled in her spot amid the trees and swiped at them all afternoon.

By sundown, Maya felt weak from hunger. She pulled the canvas bag toward her, and Artemisia took a few steps closer. She scooped a handful of the molasses grain from the bag and set it out near her feet again. Her own stomach complained. Maya considered the horse feed and sniffed it. It was just oats and grass and molasses. It wouldn't hurt her. She put a pinch in her mouth. It tasted like oatmeal with a little shredded cardboard. It wasn't entirely awful, and her stomach quieted for the first time in days. She lay back, closed her eyes, and slept.

Nightmares punished her: In a white tower, Grandmother washed her mouth out with soap. She ran to the window, jumped out, and fell, the world speeding past, her life disappearing. She found herself darting through a plain of sagebrush while a helicopter pushed her toward a net trap. She stumbled and fell. Unable to get up, she screamed while a mountain lion crawled toward her. Her father and mother swam through a pool of turquoise water to save her, but as hard as they stroked, they made no progress. Maya called to them for help. But their arms weren't long enough to reach her.

The next morning, it was more difficult to get to the river. When Maya stood, pain riveted from her foot up into her leg. This time, instead of struggling with the makeshift cane to get to the river, she scooted backward on her bottom, with her jacket beneath the stiff leg, pulling it along.

All morning, Maya watched Artemisia graze at the top of the grove, drifting closer to the ridge. She said her name from time to time, just to see her head raise in recognition. By the time the sun was directly overhead, the horse had wandered over the rise and out of Maya's sight.

"Artemisia?" Maya kept her eyes rapt at the spot where the mare had crossed over and called her repeatedly. But there was no sign of her.

Tears welled in Maya's eyes. "Please come back."

Hours later, Maya's cheeks were still damp from weeping when Artemisia reappeared. She walked into the grove as if she'd never been away, patrolled the perimeter, and stopped near a rock ledge where she peed a long stream.

"Oh, Artemisia! I'm so glad you're back. I have so much to tell you . . . and so much to ask you. . . . I need you, Artemisia. Please don't leave me again. Look! I made a fire. This time I used only the driest leaves and it worked. It took forever to get started but I finally did it. It's not a very big fire but it's enough. And I'm cooking a fish. Grandmother would have never allowed me to try, and she would not be pleased. But . . . I . . . think . . . my mother might have been proud. Do you agree?"

Artemisia paused and looked at Maya, then shook her head and made a long blow, her lips quivering.

"Do you remember her, Artemisia? She didn't give up just because Grandmother disapproved . . . and . . . neither did my father. I'm . . . I'm . . . proud of them."

Maya knew the fish was done when it began to slide off the stick. She laid it on a flat rock. The skin came off easily with a few scrapes from a broken branch. With her fingers, she pinched small bites from the fleshy areas. Maya reached into the bag and scooped out a small mound of molasses grain and piled it on the ground near the waning fire.

Artemisia walked forward and ate.

If Maya had reached out, she could have touched her neck. But she held back, afraid she'd scare the mare away. Instead, she whispered, "It's lovely to have you over for dinner. Please come again soon."

24

MAYA WAS BEGINNING TO LOSE TRACK OF HOW LONG she'd been in the aspen grove. Was it five days or six . . . or more? She retraced the days in her mind, making marks on the ground with a stick: the day of the earthquake, soaking in the river, finding the trout in the pool, the day the mosquitoes hatched, the day she had cooked the first trout, and yesterday when she cooked the second. Had she really been in the aspens an entire week?

This morning there'd been no more fish in the pool. Now, the wind blew, and she couldn't start a fire, but she didn't mind because the stiff breeze dissuaded the annoying mosquitoes.

The afternoon sky darkened. Maya felt too cold and

shivery to soak in the river. She could barely move her arm. It had grown stiffer and redder and when she touched it, the skin felt hot.

Artemisia browsed nearby, then walked into the clearing and lay down.

Was she basking in the sun or taking a nap? Maya wondered. Maybe today should be a resting day for both of them. Maya reclined in a warm stupor. Her entire body droned with soreness and warmth. She had no strength or inclination to rise, and it worried her.

Later, Artemisia lifted herself and walked to the river. She turned several times to nicker to Maya, as if asking her to come along.

"I can't. . . ." said Maya. "You go. . . ."

Thick clouds blotted the evening sky and erased the stars and the moon. "It's going to be very, very dark tonight, Artemisia," whispered Maya. "Stay close."

Sometime during the dream-laden hours between midnight and daybreak, Maya awoke to a strange cry, like the wail of a newborn baby. The sound pierced through the vale.

Artemisia snorted and made a series of high-pitched squeals.

Maya sprang upright and stared into the blackness, then heard the rousing caterwauls of a cat and a terrifying commotion: wild screeching, claws scraping on rock, hooves grating, a horse's scream, hissing, thuds on the ground, and the continuous pounding of running hooves. As fast as the fray had started, it ended with no sound at all.

A mountain lion.

Maya held her breath, her heart ricocheting. The darkness felt oppressive, and it was hard to breathe. A twig snapped. Maya jerked in the direction of the sound. Leaves crackled as something bounded through the grove. Steps came closer. Maya drew up her left knee, wrapped her arms tightly around it, and laid her head on top. She squeezed her eyes closed. "Artemisia," she whispered, "please be okay."

The wind braced. A cloud shifted, and a snip of the moon appeared.

Slowly, Maya lifted her head and saw the strange apparition. A cluster of anomalous white pieces, like a dismembered spirit, drifted before her. Maya rubbed at her eyes. She heard a nicker and soft blowing sounds. Her voice trembled and she whispered, "A ghost horse . . ."

269

But Maya wasn't afraid. There was something calming about the otherworldly being. Something graceful in the way the horse moved with a rocking motion, which almost hypnotized Maya and made her feel swaddled like a baby in her mother's arms.

As the ghost horse inched closer, its white parts grew larger. Maya watched with awe as its body emerged in its entirety, sidling so close that she could reach up and touch the underbelly.

"It *is* you," whispered Maya.

Artemisia uttered her familiar nicker.

"Was the mountain lion coming back for more? When it didn't find Klee, was it coming after you? Or me? Payton told me that mountain lions follow their prey. We . . . we have to leave this place."

Artemisia dropped her head and nuzzled Maya, her mane tickling her cheeks.

Maya reached up to stroke her warm head and neck, and this time the mare did not pull away. "Thank you," she whispered.

Throughout the night, Maya sensed Artemisia's vigilant presence. Sometimes, when Maya stirred or whimpered, she felt the mare's gentle snuffles, as if Artemisia was confirming that Maya was still safe and beathing.

"That's not good, Artemisia." Maya had removed her jacket, pulled her arm from her shirtsleeve, and unwrapped the kerchief. The wound oozed yellow. "My arm hurts worse than my ankle." Maya's face pulsed with heat and she felt achy, inside and out. She turned her troubled eyes toward the horse. "Not good . . ."

Maya managed to eat a few pinches of grain and then held out the last handful to Artemisia. As the mare nibbled from her outstretched hand, Maya looked up and considered the distance from the ground to the horse's back. Would she be able to lift herself up with an injured leg and arm? If she could sit bareback, would she be able to stand the pain of her right leg dangling without a stirrup to brace it? And what would prevent her body from slipping?

"Do you remember that you let my mother ride bareback with a Comanche Coil? Would you let me do that, Artemisia? Of course, my mother . . . my mother was completely fearless. That's what Uncle Fig said. Want to know a secret, Artemisia? I'm not completely fearless. I'm entirely afraid . . . of so many things. That you'll rear and I'll fall. Of getting lost. Of never seeing Aunt Vi and Uncle Fig and my grandpa . . . or even Payton . . . ever again . . ."

Feeble and trembling, Maya pulled the drawstring rope from the canvas bag and the drawstring from the bottom of her jacket. Then she detached the neck strap from the binoculars and made it as long as possible, tying a drawstring to each end. She spread her jacket on the ground and rolled it sleeve to sleeve, then secured one drawstring to the end of one of the sleeves. Maya struggled to stand, one-footed, and gingerly placed the rolled jacket across the withers, allowing the sleeves to drop over Artemisia's barrel. Then she waited to see if Artemisia would rear or buck.

The horse stood quiet and still and turned her head toward Maya, as if to say, "Don't worry, I remember."

Maya quickly reached under the barrel and pulled one dangling drawstring forward to meet the other and tied them together.

Maya slipped her hand under the coil and gave a gentle tug. She hopped alongside Artemisia, guiding her forward and next to a felled log. "Whoa. Okay, Artemisia. That's my girl. Please don't move." She stood on the log on her good leg, hooked her left arm and elbow over Artemisia's back, hoisted up, and dragged her right leg over, straddling the horse. The impaired right ankle hammered in agony. She felt weak and dizzy and dropped her head forward on Artemisia's neck until the light-headed feeling passed.

Artemisia shifted.

"Whoa. Whoa, girl. Now . . . I'm going to tuck my knees underneath the coil."

The left knee wedged easily. But when she tried to bend the right leg, distress sang through the lower extremity. She took a deep breath and pushed her knee forward anyway. Once her foot was supported beneath the coil, the pain eased. She slipped a hand beneath the rolled jacket at the withers.

"Okay, Artemisia. Nice and easy." Maya clucked.

Artemisia walked forward into the higher reaches of the aspen grove.

Maya glanced back at her little camp: a circle of rocks around cold ashes, a meager pile of fish bones, a pair of strapless binoculars lying on a bed of leaves, and the spot where Klee would rest forever.

Maya smiled and wept at the same time. For the leaving. And the leaving behind.

25

RIDING BAREBACK, MAYA FELT ARTEMISIA'S MUSCLES shift with every alternating step. At first, she wobbled and thought she might plummet to the ground. But soon, the inside legs and the seat of her jeans dampened with the horse's perspiration and she seemed almost fastened to Artemisia's back. A few precarious ledges worried Maya, but Artemisia walked with cautious and delicate steps. When Maya whimpered in pain, Artemisia paused until she quieted.

As they reached the crest above the aspen grove, Maya looked downriver to see that the Sweetwater had overtaken the banks, and sections of the willow were underwater. All morning, they had to circumvent mud slides and overflowing washes and ended up much farther upriver than they needed to be. They'd have to backtrack on the other side.

Maya's body teemed with pain and fever. Her head bobbled forward in a sleepy trance. But when she heard a distant whinny, she snapped alert. Was someone coming for her? "I'm here! Uncle Fig! Aunt Vi! . . . Moose!"

No one answered. A lone stallion, deep black with a white blaze and stockings, paced on the ridge opposite them and called to Artemisia.

Artemisia lifted her head and whinnied in return.

"Remington . . ." said Maya. Would he try and lure Artemisia away? The stallion kept his distance, but still Maya held tight to the coil and nudged Artemisia forward. "I need you, Artemisia . . . to cross the river and climb the mountain. To take me home."

They approached the water, and Maya looked for

shallow footing, but this part of the river was unfamiliar and rushed with a strong current. She rode for a mile until she found a calm but deep passage.

"What do you think, girl? Can we make it?" Maya clucked and pressed the horse with her knees.

Artemisia faltered before lifting and placing each hoof in the riverbed. The water soon reached Artemisia's hocks. She took deeper strides but balked midstream in front of a wide pool.

The Sweetwater toyed with Maya's feet. "We can't stop now," Maya coaxed. "Just a little farther. You can do it. Come on now." Maya held tight to the rolled coil.

Artemisia surged into the water with a floundering splash. Maya tipped sideways. Her knees released from under the coil, and she slid from Artemisia's back, splashing into the water. Maya lunged for the coil, grabbing it with one hand, and hung on. The horse swam toward the middle of the pool, dragging Maya through the river.

Maya struggled to maintain her grip. "Whoa!"

Her fist loosened. She clung with her fingers. Her head dipped underwater. Maya felt the pull of the current. She treaded wildly with her good leg and came up sputtering. "Artemisia! Whoa!"

The horse slowed in the water but sank lower.

Maya dangled at Artemisia's side. With all of the strength she could gather, she grasped the coil and pulled herself onto Artemisia's back, gripping her mane.

Artemisia swam toward land. She found the river bottom, lunged forward, and scrambled up the embankment.

Maya braced for the horse's shiver and gritted her teeth in anticipation. Artemisia shook the water from her body. Pain shot up Maya's leg. She took deep gulps of air and cried out. When the horse was still, Maya righted herself and repositioned her knees beneath the coil. Before continuing, she leaned forward and rested on Artemisia's neck until her heart and breathing calmed. She murmured, "Thank you, Artemisia . . . for getting me across."

The air cooled, and the sky turned gray. Maya looked up. The wind herded billowy rain clouds the color of soot in their direction.

Maya rode along the river, above the brush line. When the rocky outcroppings prevented passage, she forded back across the river, this time only in the shallowest of water. The Sweetwater was a zigzag of coiling turns and didn't always trickle in one direction. After a half dozen crossings and without the sun as a compass, Maya became disoriented. "Artemisia, I can't figure out which is downriver and which is upriver. I want to go down. . . ." A hawk seemed to be scouting for her as it glided above in languid loops. "Which way?" she asked.

Large rain droplets splattered on her. Within seconds, the rain pulsed from the sky. Maya dropped her head forward.

Artemisia took slow and judicious steps in the slick mud until she edged alongside an outcropping, putting their backs to the outburst.

Maya's clothes were sodden and her body ached with cold. She buried her head beneath her good arm and leaned on Artemisia's neck. And she thought about the campfire and her tepee and her sleeping bag and the truck that could get her from one place to another quickly. She thought about sandwiches, horse magazines, hot water, dry clothes, pots and pans, and plastic chairs. And even Payton's pranks. She wouldn't mind them at all right now if she could have his company.

The dark clouds thinned, the sun peeked through, and Maya reoriented to the river. The afternoon wore on until she reached the familiar gorge. Maya looked up at the steep and rocky hillside.

"Just a little farther . . ." she said. At the top she'd find the road and then it would be just another mile. She nudged Artemisia forward.

They switched back and forth across the wide mountain. Rocks had loosened from the quake, and every one of Artemisia's steps sent small cascades of dirt and pebbles toward the river. Artemisia's breathing became labored from the arduous climb. She paused and whinnied loudly.

When the horse crested the hill, Maya stopped her, sat straighter, and looked ahead, searching for any signs of movement and straining for the sound of the remuda horses. The anticipation of seeing her family began to build in her heart, tighter and tighter, like a wound-up jack-in-the-box on the verge of bursting forth.

As they continued down the road toward camp, Artemisia lifted her head higher, too. Her steps quickened.

"I know, girl. We made it."

Maya stopped Artemisia at the lookout above the campsite. Long shadows from the late afternoon sun shrouded the valley. Maya raised her hand to shield her eyes from the glare. "Do you see them, Artemisia? I can't see them." She took a deep breath and felt a strange tranquillity and happy resolve. "Hello!" she called.

There was no answer.

As she rode closer, Maya squinted. At first, she thought it was all an illusion, like a ghost horse with some parts apparent and others blending into the dark shadows. Maya swiped at her eyes in disbelief.

Everything had disappeared.

The river had overflowed and subsided. The kitchen tent, bare of any contents, stood in a bog. The office tent had vanished completely, with only a square of straw-colored grass to show where it had once stood. A stew of ashes filled the fire pit. The tepees were gone.

Maya turned Artemisia and rode up the embankment toward the corrals. Only the smaller one remained, its gate tied open. It was empty except for the water trough and a bit of hay still strewn on the ground. The other corral had been disassembled, and the ground was now littered with a few remaining round crossbars.

Maya rode Artemisia into the corral, removed her legs from the coil, and slid to the ground on her good leg. She untied the drawstrings, dragging the wadded-up jacket with her as she crawled toward the water trough. Maya leaned her head inside, drank, and rinsed her face and neck. Then she sank to the ground, putting her injured leg out straight in front of her, and leaned back against the trough.

"Where did they go, Artemisia? Did they . . . die?"

Despondent, Maya lay down, turned on her side, tucked both hands under her cheek, and cried.

As Maya traveled between consciousness and a feverish stupor, she heard her own voice singing to Aunt Vi's strumming. She squeezed her eyes tight, not wanting the delusion to end.

Down in the valley, the valley so low

Hang your head over, hear the wind blow

Hear the wind blow, dear, hear the wind blow

Hang your head over, hear the wind blow.

Roses love sunshine, violets love dew

Angels in heaven know I love you

Know I love you, dear, know I love you

Angels in heaven, know I love you.

When her dreams were silent, Maya stirred and sat up. She watched the sun straddle the horizon and then drop. The afterglow pulsed and splayed across the sky in streaks of yellow, gray, purple, orange, and pink. The air turned brisk. Her teeth chattered from the chills, and she pulled on her jacket.

Artemisia came forward and dropped her head. Maya reached up and stroked the soft muzzle. Then, with a quick jerk, Artemisia lifted her head and her ears perked.

"What is it, girl?"

Chords from a guitar lilted from somewhere in the distance.

"Did you hear that?" asked Maya. She struggled to stand and step-hopped toward the corral gate, where she paused to listen. She heard nothing. "Am I imagining things?"

Then came a clink and a clang.

"That's a bell from a hobbled horse!"

A fingering of chords tickled the air.

Maya's head swung around, trying to determine the direction of the sounds.

Artemisia's head lifted and she whinnied.

A horse answered. Then another.

"The remuda!" said Maya. "They . . . must be on the other side of the hill . . . at . . . at the old campsite. . . ."

Maya picked up a short crossbar to use as a walking stick and secured Artemisia in the corral. "You'll be safe here, girl. And I'll be back soon." Hobbling, Maya followed the road but made slow progress. She stopped when she heard the guitar again, the tones like a salve on her yearnings. She took a deep breath and smiled.

Maya looked down at herself. Dirt was packed beneath her fingernails, grime streaked her clothes, and blood stained her shirt and vest. She reached up and touched her hair. Her ponytail was long gone, and her hair was tangled and matted and stuck to her head in knots. She ran her hand over her face, now calloused from the sun and covered in scratches and bites. What would they think?

She heard another refrain from the guitar and limped closer.

When she rounded the bend, she saw the clearing with the old trailer in the background. A fire pit glowed. Four shadowy figures huddled around it. To the side, a corral enclosed the remuda horses. Maya turned her ear toward them, hoping to hear Aunt Vi's voice. But there was only the hesitant picking and strumming of heart-heavy notes.

Maya gazed at them, her body so filled up with affection and relief that tears pushed toward the surface. She wanted to be in their midst, sitting with them near the fire, listening to Uncle Fig and Moose tease each other, hearing Aunt Vi give orders, and watching Payton wrestle with Golly. Had they missed her? Or would they be angry at all the trouble and worry she had caused? Would they ever allow her to come to the Sweetwater again?

She struggled to take a step forward or to call out, but she was so strangled by her emotions that she couldn't. Maya stood silhouetted against the last gray light of dusk. She looked toward them . . . and waited to be found.

Golly saw her first. The dog's head raised and sniffed the wind. She barked and sprang in Maya's direction.

A figure stood and pointed. The others stood and their heads turned to follow Golly. For a few moments the four bodies seemed frozen. Then they all moved at once, the smaller figure racing ahead of the others, zig-zagging and jumping every few feet. She knew it was Payton. Running toward her. Closer and closer.

He stopped a few feet from her. "Maya! Is it you? We've been looking and looking. There's been helicopters and planes and search dogs and everything!"

Golly bounded around them, yelping.

Aunt Vi reached her and took her hands. She didn't seem to care that they were dirty. She kissed them anyway. "Maya! This may be the happiest day of my life!"

Maya dropped her makeshift cane and leaned into Aunt Vi's embrace and began to cry, first small sniffles and then whimpering and then sobs with hiccups.

Aunt Vi kissed her forehead. "You're burning hot with fever!"

Uncle Fig rushed up with a dish towel over his shoulder. He pulled it off and began dabbing at Maya's tears and dirty cheeks.

Their little circle opened and Moose pushed forward, his face riddled with disbelief.

Maya reached out to him. He scooped her into his arms, cradling her close.

As they all huddled together, Golly ran in circles and barked.

"Maya-bird, am I dreaming?" said Moose.

Maya wanted to say that it wasn't it dream. That it was all real and that she was so happy to be with them. And that she had missed them and thought about them every day. She wanted to tell them about Artemisia and Klee and the mountain lion. And she wanted to tell Aunt Vi she was sorry. But it was as if she had collected all of her words in a basket, and before she could share them she'd tripped, and they had all rolled away. Now as she tried to speak, she could only find one.

Maya wrapped her arms around Moose's neck and buried her head in his chest. "Grandpa."

26

Moose carried Maya into the ranch house, her arm stitched and bandaged, her foot encased in a cast. She had spent a night and a day in the hospital in a fog of X rays, procedures, anesthesia, and medications. She was so happy to be deposited into the comfort of her bed that when Golly jumped up and crept forward, Maya embraced the slobbering brown face. She sat in her bedroom, propped up by pillows like a queen holding court with her family gathered around her. That's when she told them the whole story.

"Where were you the day of the earthquake?" Maya asked.

"Payton and I had already made it back here after the dentist appointment," said Aunt Vi.

Payton grinned, showing his new tooth. "Yeah. The hanging lamps swung and the dishes walked across the table."

"Moose and I were delayed at the tack and feed store," said Uncle Fig. "A few things fell off the shelves around us, but we were none the worse for wear."

"Fig and I drove back to the campsite but found it knee-deep in water. And not a soul in sight," said Moose. "We figured you were all together, safe and sound. Aunt Vi arrived early the next morning, and we all fell into a dumbfounded scramble when we realized you were missing. A few hours later, Seltzer appeared on the hill. That's when we called in the search-and-rescue team. They brought out their big maps and marked off quadrants from here to the Red Desert. They had helicopters and small planes searching and a crew came every morning at first light with their dogs and horses and left late every afternoon. We just hadn't reached the section where you were stranded yet. But we would have, Maya," said Moose. "We would have kept looking until we found you."

Moose's eyes filled with tears but he smiled and chuckled. "Who would've guessed that you'd have to come all the way to Wyoming to feel an earthquake?"

"I didn't even know you had earthquakes here," said Maya.

"Sure," said Uncle Fig. "There was a *Terrae motus* in 1959 in Montana that was felt over half of Wyoming and all the way to Seattle. It was a doozy. 7.5! The earth from a gigantic landslide dammed a river and the thrust from all that earth falling created a wind strong enough to lift cars and trees. The geysers in Yellowstone Park spit sand —"

"Fig," interrupted Aunt Vi, "you can give her all the

details when she's rested. Maya, in a few days, I'll be heading back out to the campsite. I've got a ranch hand out there right now watching Artemisia and the horses. I need to put things in order and get set up so I can finish my summer work. As soon as that cast comes off, Moose and Fig will bring you back. Payton's going with me. Where is he? Payton!"

He popped his head out of Maya's closet. "Here I am!"

"Go outside and play with Golly," sighed Aunt Vi.

Payton ran from the room, clamoring down the stairs.

She shook her head. "We've got to get as much summer into that boy as possible. Maya, can you believe that he argued with me about going back out? He wanted to stay here with you."

Maya smiled. "I missed him, too, Aunt Vi."

On the morning they were to leave, Maya looked up to find Payton standing in the bedroom doorway.

"You can come in," she said.

He walked toward the bed, holding something behind his back. "We're leaving. Me and Aunt Vi. And well . . . I made something for you." He held out a leather drawstring bag.

Maya took it, loosened the leather ties, and peeked inside. "My horses!"

Payton shrugged his shoulders. "Your tepee flooded and the box got all wrecked. Moose taught me how to cut the leather and punch the holes and thread the cord.

"I looked and looked for the brown-and-white one and finally found it in the bushes. And I put it in your tent, but it must have gotten lost in the earthquake. It's the only one missing."

Maya shook her head and smiled. "I found it in my tent that morning right after you left with Aunt Vi. It's right here." She pulled it from the pocket of her robe. "I had it zipped in my vest the entire time I was gone." She dropped it into the bag. "I wanted to tell you thank you by finding an eagle feather for you. But I found Artemisia instead."

"That's okay. Oh, Aunt Vi says if your foot heals on time that she'll take us with her on a weekend pack trip into The Winds the last weekend of August, before I have to go home. That would be the disgusting worst if we couldn't go. So promise that you won't do something stupid to make your foot heal slow and that you'll get better really quick."

Aunt Vi called from downstairs. "Payton!"

"Promise?" he said.

Maya smiled. "I promise."

"Yes!" he said.

27

ARTEMISIA WALKED THE PERIMETER OF THE ENCLOSURE,

her instinct to keep moving still strong. It felt strange that she didn't need to wander to search for water or food. The water trough filled automatically, and someone brought hay each morning and evening for her and the other horses in the adjoining corral.

The woman came every few days to work with her, lungeing her on a long lead in a large circle. She was strict, yet gentle. Artemisia remembered the cues from a long time ago and responded to what she requested: walking, jogging, loping, backing up. Often, after a workout, the woman lingered at the corral and talked to Artemisia, just as the girl had done.

The woman groomed her, and Artemisia enjoyed being

curried and combed. Even the witches' knots and burrs disappeared from her tail and mane. After several weeks, she allowed herself to be blanketed, saddled, and tacked with a bit and bridle. Then, the woman rode her on the long track of dirt and sometimes on trails not far from the corrals.

Soon, the new routine felt familiar. Artemisia learned to recognize some of the other horses by their snuffles and blows, whinnies and snorts. But she still didn't belong to them. And they didn't belong to her.

Every evening at sunset, Remington appeared on the ridge, and when Artemisia saw him, something stirred deep within her. He whinnied and she answered, "I am here." He never approached, but wasn't consoled either, often roving back and forth until dark.

Artemisia grew accustomed to his visits. Each day by late

afternoon, she lifted her head toward the rim, searching for him and pacing in restless circles of anticipation. She didn't calm until he appeared. Every evening it was the same. The sun closed on the horizon, and she became the contented audience for his persistent wooing.

28

FOR THE SECOND TIME THAT SUMMER, MAYA SAT
between Moose and Fig in the truck cab, with Golly in
Fig's lap.

Maya leaned forward and squirmed on the seat as
Moose slowed the truck and turned onto the road to the
Sweetwater camp. It was hard to believe that it had been
more than a month since the night Moose had scooped
her into his arms and driven her to the hospital. Every
day, she had longed to be back near the river and had
missed the smell of sage, the campfires, swimming in
the river, and even her tepee. But most of all, she had
missed Aunt Vi and Artemisia. The doctor had finally
removed Maya's cast, and within days the broken ankle
became nothing more than a memory.

As they drove up the hill past the old campsite, Maya asked, "Can you let me out at the horses?"

Moose stopped the truck on the road, liberating both Maya and Golly from the cab. The dog darted down the embankment and the truck pulled away.

Maya stood on the hill, savoring the scene before her. Much looked the same: The river wound through the valley with the tall willow bushes surrounding its banks; five little tepees dotted the clearings; the office tent had been reinstated; the kitchen tent flew the flag; and a campfire beckoned.

Maya looked toward the corrals. Wilson was back, his leg healed, plus all the other horses, including Seltzer. She walked to the tack bench and ran her hands over the saddles, pads, and bridles. She had missed the smell of the leather and the damp hay. Opening the blue container, she inhaled a whiff of the molasses grain.

"Maya?"

She turned.

Aunt Vi strode forward holding a lead rope to the haltered Artemisia. The horse's brown-and-white coat had been curried and brushed to a lustrous sheen, the blond mane and tail combed sleek and smooth. Maya's heart swelled and she hurried toward them.

Aunt Vi held the rope out to Maya, and said, "She's yours now." But instead of taking the lead, Maya hugged Aunt Vi, holding her tight.

The woman rocked her back and forth. "The girl cometh back. Now we'll all be in the mush pot if we don't pull ourselves together."

Maya laughed and released her. They both had tears in their eyes.

"Hey there, girl," said Maya, taking the rope and running her hands over Artemisia's muzzle. She stroked toward her crest and down the withers and her back. Maya leaned close and nuzzled her neck.

The horse responded with a throaty nicker and dropped her head toward Maya, her mane tickling Maya's face. She rubbed her head up and down against Maya's chest, as if to say, "Welcome home."

Maya found the rhythm of camp life she had missed: rising with the aurora, hurrying to finish her chores, training on horseback until she was dusty and sweaty, and dousing in the river. As September loomed, she counted the remaining days, not wanting them to end.

Payton would be leaving soon, and she'd be heading back to the ranch with Aunt Vi, Uncle Fig, and Moose to start school.

A few days before the promised pack trip, Fig, Moose, and Payton gathered their fishing poles early in the morning and walked upriver. Golly followed. Aunt Vi and Maya watched them leave, and then looked at each other.

"Ready?" asked Aunt Vi.

Maya took a deep breath and nodded.

They walked to the corrals and tacked their horses for the trail ride they'd been discussing for days. Maya rode Artemisia, and Aunt Vi rode Seltzer and ponied Wilson on a lead rope.

They retraced Maya's journey: They picked through the shallows of the Sweetwater, surveyed the landslide from the earthquake, and dismounted in the aspen grove, tying the horses so Maya could give Aunt Vi the grand tour. Maya showed her where she had lost Seltzer, the spot Klee was buried, and the well of water in which she had found the trout. She retrieved her abandoned binoculars and demonstrated how she had made fire.

All the while, Remington shadowed them.

After they saddled up and headed home, Aunt Vi said, "He's been coming to camp every night at sunset. And when I take Artemisia out for rides, he appears. He's waiting for an opportunity. I considered letting her go, Maya, but didn't think I should make the decision."

"I'm glad you didn't," said Maya, reaching down and protectively patting Artemisia's neck.

"I know how you feel," said Aunt Vi. "If she were out there with Remington, there would always be the chance

that they'd be captured in another gather. And then separated. There's no guarantee that they'd stay free and . . .
together."

As the sun lay down on the prow of The Winds and
they headed home, Maya thought about all those days in
the aspen grove and how Artemisia had never left her.
When she looked into the blue sky warming with streaks
of orange and pink, she remembered the mountain lion
and how Artemisia had fought him off and frightened
him away. And she relived the grueling bareback journey
to camp and how carefully the horse had carried her.
Maya fixed her eyes on twilight clouds, which only a few
moments earlier had been white puffs but now drifted
across the horizon in black-and-gray silhouettes. A tear
slid down her cheek. Maya whispered, "Artemisia, we'll
always be together. . . ."

Before dark resolved, they emerged onto a vast plain with little sagebrush. Maya considered the expanse and her breath quickened. Artemisia whinnied. An irresistible desire overtook Maya, and she looked at Aunt Vi with eager query.

"Go ahead, Maya," said Aunt Vi. "Give Artemisia plenty of rein, and stay centered."

The breeze stiffened.

A sparse overture of early stars blinked. Maya clucked for the jog. Artemisia picked up speed. She kissed for the lope. Artemisia lifted and raced, horizon-bound, her hoofbeats pounding out a primal refrain, keeping pace with the beating of Maya's heart.

Who feels alive in this wind?

Artemisia huffed, her breathing loud and cadenced.

Maya heard her own voice. *Ride, Maya. Ride!* She leaned into the wind, infused with contentment for the most trivial things: the smell of sagebrush, the sound of Aunt Vi's songs, and the feel of Golly underfoot. For Uncle Fig's pancakes and a grandfather who wore his heart on his sleeve. For the ranch and her father's painting and the room with the slanted ceiling and for Payton and the promise of a little more summertime. For the parts of her that were the same and the parts of her that were new. For her mother who had traipsed all over kingdom-come on a horse. And for a journey about to begin. She rode.

Artemisia stretched into the gallop. *Hoosh, hoosh, hoosh, hoosh.*

Maya dropped the reins over the horn and held her

arms outstretched like wings. Suddenly, it was as if the ground fell away and she was no longer earthbound but galloping between emblazoned stars, faster and faster. She galloped and galloped and galloped and galloped. Time was suspended. Nothing that had happened before or might happen after mattered. She arched her face upward.

She was the horse and the stars and the wind.

Maya and Aunt Vi rode back to camp in silence. The swath of the Milky Way and the moon illuminated the horses' footfalls. Dusk settled.

Remington paced on the ridge.

Maya looked up at the stallion's silhouette. Should she let Artemisia go to him? Would his protection be enough? From a mountain lion? Or a dozen wranglers during a gather? What was the right decision? And when she decided, how would she know it was the right choice? Especially when there was so very much she didn't know about knowing.

Maya gazed at the immense panorama before her. The Sweetwater was nothing more than a wavy line of green, their campsite, one dot in the universe. But instead of feeling belittled, the bigness captured her thoughts and laid them all out, in order. *Some people get stuck and hold on much too tight. . . . You never have to get over it, you just have to get on with it. . . . Out here every single thing matters. . . . Imagine being free and then put into confinement.*

Maya slowed.

Aunt Vi continued for a short distance, then waited.

Maya turned Artemisia toward the spot where the stallion stood. She dismounted, released the cinch strap, and pulled the saddle and pads from Artemisia's back.

Remington called.

Artemisia's ears perked.

"What is it you want?" Maya whispered. "To run free and belong only to the stars . . . ?" With tender affection, she stroked Artemisia's cheek. She looked into her huge brown eye and saw her as she had the first time near the buttes: a horse her mother had ridden. With the confidence to guide. With knowledge of the land. Herd-smart and keeping peace. With shaggy hair and a knotted tail and dirt crusted on her barrel. Spirited. Alive with abandon. Maya saw her with Sargent and Mary and Georgia at the gulch, rolling in the water hole. And with Klee by her side, their necks intertwined.

Remington neighed.

Artemisia arched her head upward and answered with a hearty whinny.

Maya slipped her finger beneath the split ear bridle strap, let it drop, and slung it over her shoulder. She slapped Artemisia's thigh. "Go!" she cried. "Go!"

Artemisia started up the hill, then paused and turned toward Maya.

Maya choked on her tears. She waved her arms. "Run, Artemisia! Run!"

Artemisia bolted upward. Remington trotted to meet her. For one moment, their muzzles touched.

Remington lifted his head and whinnied.

Artemisia determined their path and he followed.

Maya held her arms high in the air and waved. And somewhere deep in her heart, a truth enveloped her, along with her tears. "We'll meet again . . . I promise . . . Artemisia."

Maya watched the two horses run across the ridge. The dark of their bodies fused with the night, and the white of their coats illuminated in an alabaster glow. Two ghostly spirits. Gossamer brushstrokes on a shadowy canvas. Jogging. Galloping. Painting the wind.

Glossary

APPALOOSA A breed of horse famed for its spotted coat.

ARABIAN A breed of horse distinguished by a small, concave yet delicate head and a long, arched neck.

AUDUBON, JOHN JAMES (1785–1851) American wildlife artist, famous for his depictions of the birds of North America.

BARREL The rounded sides of a horse, formed by the ribs.

BAY A reddish or dark brown horse with a black mane, legs, and tail.

BELLY LOOP A loop of rope around the barrel of a horse (under which the knees of a rider can be tucked and secured). Historically, used to ride bareback. In certain regions, it is sometimes referred to as a Comanche Coil.

BIT The mouthpiece of a bridle.

BLAZE A facial marking on a horse, characterized by a wide swath of white running from the forehead to the muzzle.

BLUE ROAN A horse with a black mane and tail, and black and white hairs throughout the coat, which give it a blue-gray tint.

BRIDLE A harness for the horse's head, usually meaning the head-stall, bit, and reins.

BUCKSKIN A horse with a coat the color of soft, yellowish leather, with a black mane and tail.

CASSATT, MARY (1845–1926) American painter whose parents objected to her decision to become an artist. She went on to become famous for her work with pastels. She is noted for depicting the lives of women and for her poignant portrayals of the mother-and-child relationship.

CATLIN, GEORGE (1796–1872) American painter known for his portraits of Native Americans.

CINCH A strap that goes under the barrel of the horse to secure the saddle.

COLT A young male horse not more than four years old.

CORRAL An enclosure for horses.

CURRYCOMB A flat, nubby comb, usually round or oval-shaped, for loosening dirt on a horse's coat.

DANDY BRUSH A brush, often elongated, used for making sweeping strokes across the horse's coat in order to dislodge dust and dirt.

DUN A tan-colored horse, usually with a black mane. May have circular stripes around its legs and a stripe down its spine.

EQUINE A horse or pertaining to a horse.

Equus caballus The Latin species name for horse.

FILLY A young female horse not more than four years old.

FOAL A young horse that is still nursing.

GAIT The method in which a horse moves, for example: walk, jog, lope, gallop.

GALLOP The fastest gait, about 25 to 30 miles per hour. In the wild, horses gallop when fleeing from predators or danger or to get from one place to another quickly. During the course of each stride, all four feet are off the ground.

GATHER A roundup of horses by horse wranglers or mustangers.

GENTILESCHI, ARTEMISIA (1593–1653) Italian painter of the early Baroque period. She pursued her art during a time when the artistic community did not embrace or encourage the efforts of female artists.

GRULLA A grayish-colored horse, usually with a dark mane and a stripe down its spine.

HAREM BAND A group of female horses that may include their fillies and colts (until they are two to three years old). A harem band is dominated by a stallion who does not allow any other mature male horses access to the group.

HOCK The joints in the hind legs of a horse, which correspond, more or less, to the knees in the front legs of the horse.

HOMER, WINSLOW (1836–1910) American painter, known and revered for his seascapes.

HOOF PICK A curved pick used to remove debris impacted within a horseshoe on a shod horse.

JOG A two-beat gait. At a jog, a horse travels about 6 to 8 miles per hour, about the same speed a human can run. A slow jog is easy to sit without bouncing, but during a fast jog, most riders "post," raising themselves up and down out of the saddle, in rhythm with the horse. In English disciplines, the jog is called the trot.

KLEE, PAUL (1879–1940) Swiss artist who worked with many types of media, including oil, watercolor, and ink. His art is considered difficult to classify because it has elements of many styles, including cubism, surrealism, and expressionism.

LATIGO A strap on the saddletree of a Western saddle used to secure the cinch.

LOPE A three-beat gait, about 8 to 10 miles per hour. The more extended foreleg is called "the lead." In English disciplines, the lope is called the canter.

LUNGE or LUNGEING Training or exercising a horse, usually on a long lead rope, by standing in the center of an imaginary circle and cueing the horse to move around you in different gaits.

MARE A mature female horse.

MUSTANG A wild horse.

MUZZLE The mouth, jaws, and nose of the horse.

NEIGH Also called a whinny. Usually used by horses to let others know where they are or when calling to a horse from which they've been separated.

NICKER A gentle call often used as a greeting to herd mates and sometimes to humans with whom a horse is familiar.

O'KEEFFE, GEORGIA (1887–1986) American artist noted for her symbolic depictions of landscapes, flowers, shells, and animal bones.

OVERO A horse with the overo pattern can have predominantly dark or light hair. Usually, all four legs are dark and any white markings are irregular and spattered-looking. Generally, the head markings are white, such as a bald-faced horse.

PAINT Paint horses have the confirmation of a quarter horse. It is believed that Paints are descendants of the mounts brought to what is now the American West by the Spanish conquistadors. Revered by the Native Americans for their rigor, calm disposition, and reputed magical powers, they have also been respected by cowboys and ranchers for their diligence and ability to move cattle. Typically, a Paint horse has tobiano or overo markings.

PALOMINO A white, tan, or golden color horse with ivory mane and tail.

QUARTER HORSE or AMERICAN QUARTER HORSE A breed evolved from crossing the bloodlines of Native American horses with horses of the earliest colonists from England. The quarter horse was so named because it could run a quarter of a mile faster than any other breed. It's considered a sturdy horse with a quiet temperament and is used in many disciplines.

REINS The leather straps attached to either side of a bit, by which a rider controls, curbs, or guides a horse.

REMINGTON, FREDERIC (1861–1909) American painter, sculptor, and illustrator who specialized in scenes of the American West and is notably remembered for his work in bronze statuettes.

REMUDA A group of horses from which a mount is chosen for the day and then possibly changed out on the next ride.

RIGGING RING A ring, similar to a belt buckle, on the end of the cinch through which the latigo is threaded and locked into place.

RUSSELL, CHARLES M. (1864–1926) American illustrator and painter of the American West, famous for his realistic scenes of cowboys, Native Americans, landscapes, and galloping horses. Also known for his bronze sculptures.

SADDLE PADS Soft coverings designed to protect the horse's back when saddled.

SADDLEBRED A gaited breed noted for carrying their heads high. Their bodies are usually slender and agile.

SADDLETREE The frame of a saddle, usually wooden or fiberglass.

SARGENT, JOHN SINGER (1856–1925) American painter considered the most talented portrait artist of his time. Also known for his landscapes. His work was solicited by several presidents.

SELTZER, OLAF (1877–1957) American artist whose talent was evident when he was as young as twelve years old. His art depicts the American West: cowboys, the wildlife of the Plains, Native Americans, and often common people, including immigrants.

SORREL   A standard sorrel horse has an orange body with an orange tail and mane. Also called chestnut.

STALLION   A male horse capable of breeding.

STIRRUPS   Supports hanging from the saddle to hold a rider's feet.

TACK   To put a bridle and saddle on a horse in preparation to ride.

TOBIANO   A horse with the tobiano pattern is usually distinguished by two colors: white and a darker color. Darker spots are distinctly oval or rounded and extend down the chest and neck in a shieldlike pattern. Usually, the legs are white below the hocks and knees. A tobiano horse will often have the dark color on one or both flanks. The tail can be two colors.

WALK   A slow and steady four-beat gait where the horse travels about 3 to 4 miles per hour.

WILSON, CHARLES BANKS (b. 1918)   American artist who began his career as a book illustrator. Noted for his portraits of Native Americans as well as historical scenes of the American Southwest.

WITHERS   The base of a horse's neck, the highest part of its back.

WRANGLER A cowboy, or somone on horseback who rounds up
livestock.

WYETH, N. C. (1882–1945) American painter acclaimed for his
still lifes, landscapes, and Americana murals and illustrations.
He illustrated more than twenty-five books, including edi-
tions of *The Yearling, Robinson Crusoe, Robin Hood, Kidnapped,*
and *Treasure Island.*

Information

about wild horses in America can be found at the following advocate and information agencies, and in the suggested books and videos.

Web sites

The Bureau of Land Management

www.wildhorseandburro.blm.gov

The Cloud Foundation

www.thecloudfoundation.org

The Pryor Mountain Wild Mustang Center

www.pryormustangs.org

Return to Freedom, the American Wild Horse Sanctuary

www.returntofreedom.org

Videos and DVDs

Cloud: Wild Stallion of the Rockies

Cloud's Legacy: The Wild Stallion Returns

Books for children and young adults

Mustang, Wild Spirit of the West by Marguerite Henry

Cloud: Wild Stallion of the Rockies by Ginger Kathrens

Cloud's Legacy: The Wild Stallion Returns by Ginger Kathrens

Wild Horses I Have Known by Hope Ryden

For further research

America's Last Wild Horses by Hope Ryden